FOUL PLAY & FRITILLARIES

FOUL PLAY & FRITILLARIES

LINDA JORDAN

METAMORPHOSIS PRESS

For Michael & Zoe. And also to John and the rest of my plant geeky friends for their inspiration!

TUESDAY MORNING

GINA SAT INSIDE HER NEW PRIUS C IN THE PARKING LOT OF Taylor Gardens. They were wholesale plant growers on Raven Island. Their lot consisted of crushed gravel marked out with white chalk lines for parking spaces. It was full of pickups and small cars. There were maybe a hundred, hundred-fifty spaces.

How many people worked here? It must be a larger operation than she'd thought.

She stared out through the windshield. The car's hood gleamed in the rain. The car dealer had called the color Tide Pool Pearl. Really, it was turquoise, or maybe teal. The new car was a good replacement for her old Prius which had finally died. The smaller size was nice as it made her feel a little better about all the driving she seemed to be doing these days.

Gina was trying to decide whether to bring her supplies in and lug them around. Or should she come back out to the car and get them after Mckenzie showed her around?

A few years ago she wouldn't have asked such a question.

Her age was beginning to get to her. Or perhaps it was wisdom. Gina laughed. She didn't feel wise.

Picking up her travel mug, she drank the rest of the black tea with cream inside. Such a luxury, good tea with cream.

She didn't feel confident about this job, but could definitely use the money. Her savings was slipping away as prices for everything went up and Gina worried about losing everything if she had any medical problems down the line.

But Gina had never done advertising art before. It wasn't clear what they wanted from her or whether she'd be able to produce it. She was an artist and a beginner at that. Well, enough dithering. Time to suck it up.

Gina put her rain hat on and climbed out of the car. She slipped her small purse on and opened the back door. Picked up the large bag. She hefted the bag, letting out an audible oomph, and got the straps over her shoulder. Then closed the doors and locked up.

Gina walked through the parking lot to the one-story building which housed the office. It was made of metal, like one of those temporary warehouses. An ornate wooden sign was painted with green lettering on a golden background. It read *Taylor Gardens*.

A loud noise startled her as she approached the office. Off to one end of the massive greenhouses a semi-truck roared off. On the side was painted the same sign. Or maybe it was called a logo.

She opened the half-glass, metal door and went inside. The office was sparsely decorated. Painted a stark white, with photographic posters of plant offerings from past years lining the walls. Along with large whiteboards filled with graphs and checklists. There were six metal desks, clearly bought used.

Each was topped with a computer and stacks of papers. Only three desks had people behind them, all women.

"How can I help you?" asked a rangy-looking woman in her early thirties, dressed in jeans, work boots and a green company t-shirt. Her long hair was pulled back.

"I'm Gina Wetherby, here to meet Mckenzie."

"I'll call her," said the woman. She spoke into an intercom, then looked back at Gina and said, "She should be here in a couple of minutes."

Gina nodded and set her supply bag on the floor. There was nowhere to sit. Clearly the office didn't get many visitors.

She unzipped her sky-blue raincoat. It was warm in the office.

Gina pretended to look at the posters as the woman went back to work. The other two women were dressed similarly. One with short hair, the other had long braided hair. They must all take turns in the office but spend the rest of their time out in the greenhouses.

About five minutes later, Mckenzie came in the door. Gina had only spoken to her on the phone. She was tall and muscular with short-cropped red hair and a face completely covered with freckles. Her smile was genuine and she had the sort of gray eyes that promised mischief.

"Good morning, I'm Mckenzie," she said, offering her hand.

"Hello, I'm Gina." She shook her hand.

"I called Dustin, our Marketing Manager, and let him know you're here. He'll join us when he gets here. I'll have you sign in here and put on this visitor's nametag. For safety reasons, we always keep track of who's on site. Oh, and you have closed-toed shoes on. Good. We have problems with that in the summer, people show up in sandals and it's against our rules, safety issues."

Gina signed her name and the time on the clipboard. Then put the pre-printed label on her t-shirt. She heaved her bag up and followed Mckenzie out the door.

The woman was halfway to the first greenhouse before she must have realized that Gina hadn't caught up yet. Obviously not used to giving tours or at least not used to giving them to older women loaded down with art supplies.

She slowed down and waited for Gina.

"I'll show you around, so you can get a sense of what we do here. We have the five large greenhouses you see up front and four more behind them, and our display garden is between those. Behind the greenhouses are the growing fields. We grow annuals, perennials and some bulbs. At our peak, we're shipping out 16 trucks a day. All the way up to Canada and down to Oregon. Everything is geared towards getting healthy plants out the door at their peak during the spring and early summer plant-buying season."

They stepped into the first greenhouse. It was the largest one Gina had ever seen. The ceiling had to be at least fifteen feet tall and the interior space was twice as wide. The length was about three times the height.

Instead of having an enclosed feeling, it was light and airy. The temperature was warmer than outside, but not by much. Looking up, she saw open vents, near the roof.

There were rows upon rows of black gallon-sized pots sitting on the concrete floor. All the plants looked identical. As they moved closer, she saw they were a silver-foliaged variety of lavender. There were no flowers yet, but the plants had buds.

The entire feeling of the place was like a factory, not a garden. Seeing all those quite charming lavender plants en masse made them much less appealing.

There was a man at the far end, who was bent over and checking something about a plant. He moved on farther down the row to check another one.

"We have these plants inside, even though they'd be happy outside. We're giving them just a little extra heat, which has made them bud up. Keeping the rain off them helps too, otherwise they'd be sulking and droopy. They like a little dryness. They'll ship out in a few weeks. As soon as the buds color up and begin to open. They'll be on the shelves at all the big-box stores, blooming, a couple of months earlier than they would in someone's garden. But most people don't shop for plants in July, so we push them into blooming earlier."

Gina nodded and they continued on through to the middle of the greenhouse. There was a large walkway going crosswise. A piece of heavy equipment was parked on part of it. One that looked like it could lift pallets, even though Gina saw no pallets in this greenhouse.

They walked to the next greenhouse on the right. There were doors which looked like they'd could be closed but were now open. Gina could see into the next greenhouse and it was the same. So were the ones behind her. Everything looked open and one could walk, or drive, between all the greenhouses without opening and closing doors.

The next one felt noticeably warmer and was filled with annuals. Mixed baskets in pink and orange pots. The pink ones had pink plastic handles which hung from a line. The line was moving and at one point had a watering wand attached to it. It sprinkled the pot beneath it, the pot moved on and the next one stopped beneath the wand, which watered it. Gina mused over all the possible malfunctions, but still, it was an ingenious system.

The water which dripped out of the bottom of the pots was collected in a channel that ran through the concrete to a drain. It wasn't falling on the plants on the floor.

"We sometimes add fertilizer to the water and all our water is collected, filtered and recirculated. The water is tested regularly so we're not over-fertilizing plants. They all have different needs."

"What about pesticides?" asked Gina. "We all want to keep bees alive."

"We use them sparingly. We never use neonicotinoids, they're bad for the whole environment, not just the bees. We've been using beneficial insects for about five years now. They've cut our pesticide use by seventy percent. We decided to keep adding more. And when we find a problem, we close off the greenhouse and work on dealing with the problem as quickly as possible, using the least invasive means we can. It's a problem, because many of our greenhouses are a monoculture. Our Production Manager, Angie Taylor, is really committed to making our production ecologically sound."

There were more people visible near this greenhouse, one was on a large machine's lift, checking the hanging plants. Two more were working on the pots on the floor, cleaning them up. Another was loading up some of the floor pots into short plastic crates sitting on another pallet- loader like the one she'd seen parked in the first greenhouse.

A woman with an electronic tablet stood staring at the plants then began typing on it with both hands. Gina never could text or type with her left hand.

"These pots will be shipping in two weeks. This greenhouse will be empty in three weeks. Ready for some of the field plants to come in and prepare to ship."

A handsome-looking man in jeans and a tan sports jacket came in through the far door. His clothes looked out of place in this environment, even though his brown hair looked windblown and slightly disheveled.

He walked over to the woman with the tablet and put his arm around her. Then spoke into her ear. The woman looked very uncomfortable with his attention.

Then the man came over to talk to Mckenzie and Gina.

"Hello," he said, holding out his hand. "I'm Dustin Taylor, you must be Gina."

"Hello," she said, shaking his warm hand.

"Mckenzie, go contact Mariah about the open house. She has a lot of questions. I've got too many other things to deal with today."

Mckenzie looked confused, then said, "Sure. It was nice meeting you in person, Gina. You can check in with me on the days when you come here to work."

"I'll do that," said Gina.

Mckenzie walked back towards the office. Gina felt sure the woman had thought she was going to continue to tour around once Dustin arrived.

Gina clearly wasn't the only one put off by his manner.

They continued walking through the greenhouses, back towards the center one, which lay directly behind the office.

"Well, so you're going to design our new labels and tags. That's terrific. Dad, Bob, really loves your work. He's thinking your art will give us a look that will stand out from our competitors. Make people pick up the plant and buy it," said Dustin.

"And you don't agree," she said.

"I don't know. I think a photograph of the plant might be a better choice. But Bob had been doing this longer than I have. Even though us kids run it, the company is Dad's. He built it. And my brother Cory, our General Manager, who we should see around here somewhere, he likes the idea of paintings too."

"I just had a brief conversation with Bob. He told me to come and take a look around. I don't really know what you're looking for," said Gina.

Dustin seemed annoyed. Gina didn't like to ruffle people's feathers, but she'd learned long ago to stand up for herself. Otherwise people walked all over her.

"I don't know what to say to that," he said. "I thought you and Bob had agreed to everything."

"I agreed to come out and take a look at things and give it a try. Tell me what you want."

"I want marketing material. I want a plant tag, and in some cases, a label we'll glue to the pot, that shows the plant at its peak. I want artwork that'll instantly tell someone that we grow quality plants. Something that after they see the tag or label a couple of times, they'll associate with plants that perform. Something that will create repeat purchases. Even customers who will seek out our plants every time they walk into the store. We're selling the dream of a beautiful garden. I know it's asking a lot," he said, grinning.

"Yes, it is. I can paint what the plants look like at their peak, but it might not be the style you want. A painting isn't a photograph."

"I realize that. But if there's enough similarity between them and we have our logo on the tags, it might be enough to brand us. We do have a brand already, but Cory's right. Everyone's gone to photographs. We want to stand out. We need to reinvent our brand."

They'd passed into the last greenhouse on the far side. Inside this one was a shipping factory. A conveyer belt filled with pots of blooming tulips. People stood along it, trimming off any dead flowers or broken stems. Other people checked to make sure each pot had a plant tag in it.

Then the pots were put into plastic crates on a piece of machinery. When the crate was full, someone drove the machine over to a wall of tall rolling carts. The crate was transferred onto the cart. When the cart was full, it was pushed over towards the large open doors. Each cart looked like it contained different plants. And the carts looked like they were grouped by truckloads. Probably going to different stores and filling particular orders. At the far end, several carts were being pushed and pulled up a ramp into a truck.

There was an enclosed office at the opposite end. The door was opened and a short man came out. He was wearing the company t-shirt.

He yelled, "This isn't the end of it!" Then slammed the door. His face red and twisted with fury. He glanced into the warehouse, his eyes lingering on Dustin.

The man pointed to Dustin and yelled, "You're going to pay, you bastard!" Then he stomped out through the large open door.

Dustin watched the scene, as did the other workers in the greenhouse, but Gina couldn't make out from his expression what he thought about it.

Then another man came out through the closed door. He looked older than most of the workers, who seemed to be in their twenties or thirties. He was on the plump side with a belly that made the loose company shirt bulge slightly. His face looked creased with worry and frustration.

"Cory," said Dustin, loudly. "I want you to meet Gina Wetherby.

The man's face immediately changed to one of delight.

"Hello, I'm so pleased to meet you. I really hope you'll agree to paint our new tags," said Cory, holding his hand out to shake hers.

"Hello," said Gina. "I had no idea you folks grew so many plants."

"We do. It amazes me. I remember when I was a kid and Dad only had two small greenhouses," said Cory, grinning. "Let me grab you a few plant tags and labels, so you can see what we're doing now."

Cory went to a rack, made of square black plant pots on their sides, each slanted slightly upwards. They were filled with plant tags. He pulled three different tags out, then from another rack, took several four-inch round labels.

One label showed a group of annuals, an orange flax, a purple coleus and a multi-shaded orange and yellow petunia. It was a striking combination that screamed color and passion. Her friend, Melanie, would love it. Gina preferred more subtle combinations for her own garden, but this was definitely in style.

Around the edges of all the tags and labels was the same border in gold and green with a logo for Taylor Gardens that had a silhouette of a flower plus the words, *TAYLOR GARDENS: Come Garden with Us.*

"You want art that fits into the template, I'm assuming," said Gina.

"Yes, that general shape. For these we started with larger photos and then shrank them down to size," said Dustin. "depending on whether they were for a label that went on the outside of the pot or the tag stuck inside the pot."

"How about I do a few quick watercolors for you and you decide if you think they'll fit," said Gina.

"You're not sure they will?" asked Cory.

"I've never done advertising art before," said Gina.

An older man came up to them. Bob Taylor. She ran into him every now and then around town. That's how this idea had come about in the first place.

"Good morning, all," he said, radiating a bubble of enthusiasm and happiness, like he always did. "What are you all conferring about?"

Cory began to explain.

There was noise on the other side of the warehouse. People were running to hide. A man had walked in the doorway.

The short man who'd stomped out earlier.

He carried a rifle. Raised it to shoot.

Gina yelled, "Look out!"

She ran behind a large pallet-loading machine. The others scattered. There was gunfire.

Gina pulled out her cell phone and called 911.

"911, what's your emergency?"

"A man shooting. At Taylor Gardens. Hurry," she whispered.

"Are you in a safe place?"

"No. I can't talk. Please hurry," she whispered.

She hung up. More shots fired. Screaming and yelling. Gina couldn't make out any words. She was afraid to move.

Her heart raced. She breathed deeply. Think.

She needed to listen. Everything was silent now. Was the man still there? Who was he trying to kill? Cory or Dustin? Maybe even Bob.

She remembered seeing the man walk in through the door, past the other employees. Paying them no attention as they scattered. No, he'd been looking at the group of people she was in.

But he might not be satisfied once he'd killed whoever he was after. That man had been full of rage when he first left the building.

She glanced around, but everything was out in the open behind her. She'd found the only hiding spot for yards. Gina stayed still, squatting down behind the machine.

Even if she made it to the other greenhouses, there was nothing to hide behind. It was all clear glass with plants that were only a foot tall. Nowhere to hide there.

She put her bag of supplies down. Then peered out from behind the machine. She couldn't see him. Her heart pounded.

Gina could see another woman hiding behind the conveyor belt. She had a rosary out and was praying.

In the distance there were sirens. She heard footsteps. Running. It could be anybody.

She couldn't see the doorway or anyone.

The sirens grew louder.

It seemed to take forever before Gina saw people wearing the black uniforms of the Raven Island Police. They crept along the machinery keeping under cover.

She recognized Deputy Hammond nearby. The woman's hair was short again and she made eye contact with Gina who kept her face noncommittal, shrugging her shoulders. She could tell the Deputy nothing.

The Deputy moved forward out of Gina's sight, as did the other officers.

It seemed to take a very long time. And Gina heard another siren.

"Clear," said someone finally. "Get that stretcher in here."

She heard people begin to talk and was about to try to stand up when Deputy Hammond came past and held out her hand.

"The shooter's gone now. Are you all right?"

"I don't know. I'm not shot, at least."

Gina took the deputy's hand and tried to straighten her legs. How had she even done that? She hadn't know it was possible for her to still squat. Her knees weren't what they used to be.

"What happened?"

Gina described the situation.

"Do you know his name?"

"No, but he worked here. He had on the company t-shirt at least. You could ask Dustin. He pointed at him as he left, the first time."

"Dustin is who?"

"He's the Marketing Manager. Dustin Taylor."

"Ah, I'm afraid he's been shot."

"Oh no," said Gina.

She glanced over towards the door. Paramedics were wheeling a stretcher out. Bob stood in the doorway, visibly sobbing. He was being held by Cory and the tall rangy woman Gina had seen in the office.

"Will he be all right?" asked Gina.

"He's dead," said the Deputy, shaking her head. "Did you know him?"

"I just met him this morning. And there's no sign of the gunman?"

Deputy Hammond shook her head.

Gina took a deep breath and let it out slowly. What a terrible mess. She felt so badly for Bob. What must it be like to lose his son?

TUESDAY AFTERNOON

NEARLY EVERYONE WAS HERDED INTO THE STAFF BREAK ROOM TO wait. It was a too-small windowless room in front of one of the greenhouses. It smelled like coffee and sweaty bodies. There were just enough chairs. Bob, Cory and the rangy woman weren't there. They must be waiting elsewhere.

The walls were a dingy off-white, cluttered with official notices about regulations and governmental workplace rules, in Spanish and English. There were two refrigerators and a coffeemaker near a sink. Hooks on the wall held a plethora of unmatched mugs. Along with a large sign that read: *Clean up after yourself.* Signs on the refrigerators read: *This refrigerator is cleaned out every Sunday. Any food left in it will be tossed.* and *Please only take food that you brought.* A vending machine with water and sodas stood against one wall.

About forty people were jammed into the room. Gina wondered if there were more employees here today. It seemed like a small amount. Perhaps there was another room in one of the other buildings.

15

Two women were quietly talking while making coffee over near the sink. Another woman stood in the corner and was talking on her cell phone. Gina recognized her from the office this morning. It sounded like she was ordering pizzas.

The clock on the wall said 12:16. Lunch time.

Gina sat at a small table with Mckenzie, the young woman who Dustin had embraced and two men. No one was speaking.

Every now and then, one of the deputies would call someone and since they didn't return, Gina assumed they were sent home. The police were probably closing the business for the day.

The older of the two men, perhaps in his fifties, sat directly across from her. His face, tan and weathered from working a lifetime in agriculture, looked anxious.

"Jason, calm down," said the young woman to his right.

"I can't. Those plants need watering and no one's going to do it. And if we don't get the shipments out the door today, we'll be behind. Which means more plants to water and deliveries not made. And no empty greenhouses to prep the next deliveries in."

"Jason, Dustin's dead."

"Ask me if I care," said Jason, staring at her. "I know you don't either, Sarah, the way he was always bothering you. He was scum."

Gina wasn't shocked at his assessment of Dustin. Given more time with him, she probably would have come to the same conclusion.

Sarah blushed. "I wouldn't wish him dead. Just somewhere else."

"I'll be you wished you hadn't come here today," said Mckenzie to Gina.

"Well, I hadn't planned on this."

"It's just terrible. I feel so sorry for Bob. And Angie and Cory."

"Who was the man who came in with the gun?"

"That was Carlos Martinez. Both he and his daughter worked here. She quit last week. Got a job with a nursery over in Stanwood."

"He seemed to be having an argument with Cory. But then as he left the first time, he pointed at Dustin. Do you know what that was about?"

Mckenzie shook her head.

"Probably the usual," said Jason.

Gina looked at him.

"Dustin couldn't keep it in his pants," said Jason. "Pardon me, Ma'am, but it's the truth. You used to be close to Lucia, Mckenzie."

"She never said anything about him to me, but she wouldn't have. He's my ... was, my boss," said Mckenzie.

"And he never came on to you?" asked Jason.

"He tried. I told him I was gay. And very married. That shut him down. He didn't believe it though, until he saw us out at the Marina one evening, celebrating Steph's birthday. Since then he's given me the cold shoulder."

The door opened and Cory came in. The room dropped into silence.

"Hi everyone. We don't really know what happened yet, but it looks like Carlos Martinez shot and killed Dustin. We think he left after that. The police have searched nearly all of the property. His truck's gone. Angie's taken Bob home. She won't be back today. The police want to talk to everyone who was here on-site. Then you'll be let go for the day. I don't know when we'll reopen. Hopefully tomorrow. There are shipments that need to go out, but the police have to finish investigating. I told Carla to order pizza for everyone. When will they be here?"

"Fifteen minutes, from now," said Carla. She was the woman Gina recognized from the front office.

"So, have some pizza. When the police release you, get your belongings and go home. We'll let you know when we can reopen. You'll all be paid for a full day, of course."

Cory looked as if he were carrying a very heavy load. He went back out the door and conversations resumed.

Gina's stomach growled. She'd brought her lunch, but it was still in her supply bag, which she'd left out near the pallet-loading machine. She'd get it after talking to the police.

The pizza arrived before Gina was called for her interview by the police. It was from Corvid Pizza. She recognized the raven logo on the boxes.

Gina took two slices of the Mediterranean, those were her favorite. There were bottles of water and several types of soda. She chose water and drank half of it before eating.

The room grew silent as people ate. The mozzarella, tomato sauce and basil flavors calmed her. The crust was perfect, not mushy, just a bit of crunch, like good French bread.

Corvid had the best pizza, she just wished the circumstances were different. The flavor of the melted cheeses was accented by their herbaceous tomato sauce and fresh basil on top. She could at least smile inside.

Still, even if the job still existed, Gina was debating whether she want to work here. She'd already been closer than was comfortable to two murder investigations in the last couple of years. This one at least, it seemed clear who the murderer was, just not whether they acted alone.

But that wouldn't dampen the emotions of everyone around the victim. Losing someone you cared about, or who was important upset the whole apple cart. And even though the people she'd talked to didn't seem to particularly like Dustin, he was important to the company.

His death opened up the position of Marketing Manager. Someone had to fill it, if even temporarily. The work had to get done. And she'd be working with that person.

The door opened just as Gina finished her pizza.

A deputy came in and said, "Gina Wetherby."

Gina stood and tossed the empty plate and napkin. She brought the water with her.

The Deputy led her to the office that was just off where Dustin had been killed. The greenhouse space had been taped off and two people in white suits with hoods and gloves were squatting down. Probably collecting evidence.

Inside the small office sat Deputy Hammond and Sheriff Jannson. There was a cluttered desk with a computer on one side of the room. The other end held five smallish upholstered chairs circled around a table. The place smelled of pizza. They'd probably had the same lunch.

"Gina, come sit down," said Sheriff Jannson. "And tell my why it is that you keep showing up wherever there's a murder in my county."

He held up her bag of supplies. His face looked half-amused, half-annoyed and his right eyebrow was crooked.

She couldn't tell which half reigned, the amusement or annoyance. They'd known each other for a couple of years now and gone out on a sort of date, two weeks ago. They'd gone for dessert, tea and coffee at a local cafe and had planned on meeting again, but his schedule had suddenly gone ballistic.

"You found it, thank you," she said, taking her bag. "I'd sure like to stop turning up where there's a murder, I can tell you."

Gina sat down in the small chair.

"Now, tell me what you're doing here and when you arrived and what happened," said the sheriff.

"Bob wants me to do their new plant labels and tags."

"A bit late in the season for that isn't it?" he asked.

"For next year. I haven't decided yet. He asked me to come and look around, talk to people, see what I thought. I've never been here, so I agreed. I got here and met Mckenzie who was showing me around."

She related the rest of the morning to him, including what had looked like Dustin's unwanted advances to Sarah and then the gunman coming in the door and Gina calling 911.

"So you called it in?" asked the sheriff.

"Yes. I couldn't stay on the line. It was deadly silent in there and I didn't want to draw attention to myself. I was trying to hide."

"Were you hiding where your bag was found?" he asked, nodding at her art supply bag.

"Yes, not a great place, but it was all there was."

"Have you met anyone here before today?"

"Well, I've known Bob for years, but none of his kids. And I spoke to Mckenzie on the phone a couple of days ago, to set up coming this morning."

"But not Dustin."

"No."

She relayed what she'd heard in the break room.

"Do you know what position Jason has here?"

"No, not a clue. He's older though. I think most of the people who work here seem to be in their twenties and thirties. I'd guess he's at least fifty."

The sheriff nodded.

"So, you're not sure if you want to take the job?"

"No, I'm not."

"But you might want to."

"I might. Why?"

"Well, I've heard some things that make me think that this isn't as simple as it looks. If you were to work here, I'd be grateful if you kept your ears and eyes open."

"Why me?"

"You're trustworthy. People like you and they confide in you."

"Is it safe?" she asked.

"Well, Carlos won't be back. We picked him up and he's being charged. If I think it's no longer safe, I'll tell you."

"Fair enough. Okay, I'll take the job."

"Thanks, I owe you one."

"You'll owe me three. Don't think I've forgotten the other cases."

He laughed. Deputy Hammond grinned. She'd been on those cases as well.

"Can you tell me what you've heard that makes you think something's not clear?" she asked.

"My replacement, Sheriff Winters, arrested Mr. Martinez. Winters gave me the information about half an hour ago."

"Your replacement? Why are you being replaced?" Gina asked.

"I'm retiring in a month."

He hadn't told her that. Had something happened in the last two weeks?

"And Deputy Hammond won't become Sheriff?" Gina asked, and realized the question was inappropriate. She had no idea how those things worked.

"I have no desire whatsoever to be Sheriff," said Deputy Hammond. "I don't want that much responsibility. Sheriff Winters is extremely competent and just needs to get a feel for this part of the country. Chicago is a completely different place."

"He's from Chicago?"

"She," said Deputy Hammond.

"Wonderful. We need more women police," said Gina.

The Sheriff and Deputy nodded.

"I think we're done with you," said Sheriff Jansson. "Cory asked you to stop by the front office on your way out."

"Is he still here? He should have left."

"He's trying to deal with the fallout of being closed for the day. It's messed up their entire shipping and delivery schedule," said the Sheriff. "On top of everything else."

Gina nodded. She could imagine what a jumble things were just as they were ramping up for their busy season.

"I'll be in touch," said the Sheriff. "If there's anything you think I should know, call me or Deputy Hammond."

"Okay, I will," said Gina. She stood and picked up her bag of art supplies.

One of the deputies walked her out to the front office. Cory was the only one there, sitting at a desk and typing on the keyboard.

"Oh, hello Gina. What a mess."

"I'm so very sorry," she said.

"Thank you. I haven't begun to deal with it. I probably won't until I get home. I'm too busy juggling the schedule. Trying to get the plants to the stores while they're still at their peak. We work so hard to time things down to the day. So losing a day of work messes everything up. But here I am jabbering on and this is your first time here. We haven't made a good impression, I think. I'm sorry for that."

"Nothing you could have done about that," she said.

"Well, I knew Dustin had a wandering eye. I didn't realize things had gone so far and I should have. I should have warned him and then fired him. Just like every other employee here. We don't tolerate abuse of any kind and I'm ashamed to say it was my own brother."

"Could you have fired him?"

"No, but I should have done something. Not even realizing was foolish. I was just too busy."

"You can't expect perfection. From anyone or from yourself. You need to forgive yourself for that."

"If I had known, Dustin might still be alive."

"You don't know that. And you can't carry that. You didn't kill him."

Cory rubbed his face.

"You're right. You're saying all the things I'd tell one of my workers in the same situation. But it doesn't make the feelings go away. I'm tired and grieving. Emotionally a disaster area."

"You need to finish up quickly and go home."

"You're right again," he said. "How did you get so smart."

"Age," she said.

"Not everyone who's older is wise."

"No, but I was very foolish in my younger years. I have no other answer for you."

"I hope you'll come back. I hope you'll agree to do our labeling. I think it would be a great partnership. We like to support local businesses."

"I think I will. I need to consider what I have to offer."

"We'll be back up and running tomorrow. I don't know who will be here. And I don't know who our new Marketing Manager will be. I haven't given that any thought. Angie and I will need to get together and make a decision. Talk to those working with Dustin and see what's needed. But I can guarantee you that you'll have the spot for the artist. Both Angie and I love your paintings."

"I haven't met Angie," said Gina.

"She's our Production Manager. A brilliant plantsperson. She's tall and wears her long brown hair tied back. Angie might have been in the office when you arrived this morning. She was going to put in orders for next year's seeds and plants."

"Oh, I might have talked to her then."

"I'll introduce you when you return."

"I'll be here, day after tomorrow. I'm sure tomorrow will be chaotic."

"Good plan. I'm sure you're right. See you then."

Gina walked out into the rain. She didn't bother with her hat. The drizzle felt cleansing. A relief after the stress of the morning.

What would Thursday be like? She still wasn't sure her

paintings would sell plants, but she'd give it a try. She'd stuck some of the tags and labels inside her supply bag. She'd work on those tomorrow.

Then Thursday, she'd return to paint. And see if there was a new Marketing Manager.

THURSDAY MORNING

Gina arrived at Taylor Gardens at nine. Many of the workers came to work as early as seven, but she valued her retirement and the gift of sleeping in.

It was a cloudy day. There might be rain later today or tonight. The wind was brisk, coming off the Sound which lay a mile or two off to the south. She could smell the salt and kelp, even from this distance.

Inside the office, three people were using the computers and another bustled around, with piles of paper. Another was on the phone, pacing back and forth near the wall.

Mckenzie was one of those at a computer. She glanced up when Gina came in and said, "Hi Gina. I'll be with you in a minute. Just need to finish this email."

Gina nodded. She signed in on the visitor's clipboard and filled out a name tag, sticking it onto her long-sleeved t-shirt.

The pacing woman was the tall rangy one. She must be Angie, the other Taylor sibling. She ended her phone call, looking frustrated.

She walked up to Gina, held out her hand and said, "You must be Gina, the artist. I'm Angie Taylor."

Gina shook hands and said, "Nice to meet you. I'm so sorry about Dustin."

"Thank you. It's been a nightmare dealing with the morgue, the police and now the funeral home. I'm so much better with plants. And people who talk plants."

Gina laughed, "I know what you mean."

"I'm glad you're considering being our artist. I think we're due for a big change in our packaging. I love your work. It'll be an honor working with you."

"Thank you," said Gina.

Normally, she'd feel embarrassed, but Gina could tell Angie wasn't trying to butter her up. The woman was being honest and wasn't smooth, like her brother Dustin had been. It was a relief.

Mckenzie got up from her desk and walked over.

"Well, I'd better get back to work. We've got so many things to adjust. Lowering temperatures in some greenhouses to slow some plants down a bit. Gotta make sure we're adjusting the production line to make up for things," said Angie.

Gina nodded.

Angie left the office through the back door, which Gina hadn't noticed before.

"I'm so pleased you're back," said Mckenzie. "Let's go to the break room. I need to grab some coffee. And I can tell you what we've got planned."

Gina followed Mckenzie out through the back door this time. It led directly into a covered tunnel that went into the area where the break room was.

The room was empty. Tables were littered with morning papers and a few empty used mugs.

"Everyone's gotten sloppy," said Mckenzie, clearing one table, putting the mugs in the sink and the newspapers in a pile on another table.

Gina put her art supply bag on an empty chair and sat down, slipping her jacket off onto the back of the chair.

Mckenzie poured a cup of coffee and asked, "Do you want anything in it?"

"Oh, no thank you. I don't need any coffee this morning," said Gina. "I have a thermos of tea."

She pulled out her travel mug and sipped some strong Irish breakfast tea. The full flavor of the black tea melded perfectly with rich cream. She savored the taste. Mckenzie sat down next to her.

"Well, first thing, I've been chosen to be the new Marketing Manager."

"Congratulations, that's wonderful."

"Well, maybe. I'm happy about it, but I'm overwhelmed."

"I think you were already doing most of the work before this, weren't you?"

"I was. Dustin liked to dump everything on my plate. So, I know how to do the organizing and planning part of the job. I'm good at that. It's the schmoozing I fail at," said Mckenzie.

"Everyone has a different style. I suspect Dustin excelled at schmoozing, but you know, that's probably an outdated style. One that works for good old boys but doesn't work for young women. When women do that, it's taken as flirtation. Sexism is still alive and well in the business world I'm sure. When I was a marketing manager for a line of gift shops, perhaps ten years ago, it certainly was. Not for me, I was over forty and therefore, invisible. But I watched some of the young women using that style. It worked for them, for a short time, until some guy came along who wanted to act on what he considered flirting."

"What did you do?"

"I had to invent my own style. Play to my own strengths. I was confident about my ability to honestly talk to people and I had an artistic eye. I used those wherever possible. It didn't always work, but neither does schmoozing."

Mckenzie nodded.

Gina said, "You strike me as honest and straightforward. That's a welcome thing in sales. And if you know the product you're selling, backwards and forwards, and are trying to genuinely help the person you're selling to then that's gold."

"Good. I've got more learning about plants to do. They keep coming up with new ones, but it's a relief I don't have to be Dustin. Because I can't be."

"I think the world is full, up to here, of men like Dustin. At least all the women I know are sick of them," said Gina.

"The women I know are too. But I hang out with people who are more alternative."

"Well, people's beliefs are shifting and I like to think, for the better."

"Good. Well, we're looking to have tags and labels for next year printed at least by January. Angie's already put in our orders for next year, so I can give you a partial plant list today. Some of the plants will be put into mixed containers and that list will be ready by next week. The lists will give you a place to start. We're at the beginning of spring which means things will begin shipping out quickly, very soon. The bulk of the plants will be gone by the end of May. I don't know how many you can paint each day."

"I often paint from photos that I take."

"Oh, good," said Mckenzie, looking relieved. "Then you can go around taking photos of everything before they go out. I can get you a list of what's shipping each week. We probably should have gotten this started last month, but you've only missed a week's worth of shipments and we still have the same plants. They're waiting to be shipped out. So if you get good photos of everything and then paint what you can, when you can, you'll catch everything. The only things that will be missing will be next year's new plants and new mixed baskets. We can get you photos of those plants, but you'd have to imagine the mixed baskets. Would that work for you?"

"I'll think about if there's a better way," said Gina. "I can probably do it. Depends on if I'm familiar with the plants."

"Well we can leave those for last. You could at least see the plants growing, but not in bloom."

"That would help," said Gina. "Photos hide small details."

"Okay, we'll let's get a list from Cory. If you want, you could leave your bag in his office. His door is open to everyone. And that way you won't have to haul it around everywhere. It looks heavy."

"It is. I'd like to leave it somewhere close, but out of everyone's way. His office is a good choice, I think."

Mckenzie drained her coffee, then washed the mug and put it in the drying rack. They left the room and walked down the corridor to the shipping greenhouse.

Cory wasn't in his office. Mckenzie sat down at his desk and brought up the lists of plants and their projected shipping dates. She began printing them out.

Gina stood in front of the large metal bookshelves which lined one wall, amazed at the number of books. Everything from pesticide use to organic culture methods to plant encyclopedias. It was a rather extensive library. Although there were few actual gardening books, about how to use plants in the landscape. Her friend, Melanie, had an entire bookcase of those. But Melanie was a gardener, as well as a propagator, for a small collector's nursery, Ravenswood. Gina had often painted there.

"Okay, let's go out and find the first group of plants for you," said Mckenzie. "And I don't think you ever got a chance to see our display garden."

"No, I didn't."

Gina left her art supplies against the wall just inside the door and followed Mckenzie through two greenhouses. In the center of all the greenhouses was an outdoor garden. It had yellow bricks laid out in an intricate pattern and a large modern copper gazebo. Some of the side panels and the top were filled with etched glass.

The patio area was surrounded by a labyrinth of raised garden beds, the soil mostly bare this early in the season. Spring bulbs were poking through the soil in places. A few of the early daffodils were blooming.

"The beds closest to the courtyard belong to Angie. She creates the most dramatic designs there. I love seeing what she does each year. The outer beds are designed by the wholesale companies we buy plants from. They're our trial gardens. They all get the same maintenance and in June we have an open house. The wholesalers can see what the plants do in our climate. Each company has the option to have both a sunny spot and a shaded area over under the trees there."

Mckenzie pointed to raised beds beneath a row of Japanese maples, leafed out in colors of spring green, peach and pale-pinkish green. Perennials were growing there already. Varieties of green leaves with white speckles or streaks, *Pulmonaria* also had pink, blue and even white flowers. Amber and green-leafed *Heuchera* and the green leaves of foxgloves mingled in some of the shade beds.

"Are most of the trial beds annuals?" asked Gina.

"Yes. Only a few companies have perennials and most of those aren't up yet. It's good to see it now and compare it to what you'll see in June. You might want to paint it then and do some sort of border we could use for marketing."

"I love painting gardens, but I do it in a completely different style than the botanical paintings."

"Well, let's see what you think, come June. I think you might like it."

They continued on to another greenhouse. Inside it stood Angie and Cory, talking about the plants nearest them. They waved, but didn't come over.

"These are the bulbs you'll want to get photos of today. We've already shipped most of them, but held a few back so late shoppers could still enjoy spring bulbs," said Mckenzie.

The floor was filled with pots of several varieties of daffodils, tulips and a plant that Gina knew she should know the name of, but it wasn't coming to her.

"What are those?" Gina asked.

"*Fritillaria imperialis*, crown imperial fritillary. I just learned that last month. I love the way they look with their fluffy tops."

There were three long rows of them. Two foot tall plants with flowers in orange-red, orange or yellow. The plants had whorls of leaves up to a foot, then bare stems for the next foot, topped with a flurry of bright bell-shaped blossoms. A fluff of green leaves sprayed out above the flowers. The smell nearest them was slightly skunky.

"Once they're in the ground, they'll eventually get to 3' tall. I love such bright colors in our dreary spring," said Mckenzie. "And they do smell, apparently like fox urine. Which is supposedly a deer and rabbit repellent. So, bonus."

"They really are something else," said Gina.

"And in the next greenhouse we have more *Fritillaria*. We're moving into experimenting with more bulbs this year, seeing if customers will buy them. These are the gaudy fritillaries."

The greenhouse grew suddenly darker.

Gina glanced up. The pots hanging on the line above weren't blooming and looked small. Probably would peak later in the season. Beyond them, charcoal-colored clouds blackened the sky.

She followed Mckenzie into the next greenhouse. The pots here were smaller, four-inch sized. Half of the pots had flowers that were white and others a deep dark purple.

"These are *Fritillaria meleagris*, checkerboard fritillaries. And those are *Fritillaria michailovskyi*."

Mckenzie pointed to plants that had diminutive brownish-purple bell shaped flowers with yellow ruffles at the bottom of each blossom. The foliage of all the fritillaries in this room looked grasslike.

At the far end of the greenhouse, a worker was on a mechanical lift, adjusting something concerning the line of overhead pots. The baskets were made of wood and probably contained fuchsias. Gina recognized the man, but didn't know his name. She supposed the water lines would need adjustment as to the ratio of fertilizer put in it, depending on the plants being watered.

Mckenzie took Gina to a third greenhouse filled with small pots of short *Iris reticulata*, grape hyacinths and crocus. All of them showing blooms.

Rain pelted down on the greenhouse roof, creating a noise Gina was familiar with. The downpour got heavier and soon the noise was deafening.

"This is the last bulb greenhouse. So you'll want to take photos of these three greenhouses today. The plants will all be gone by the end of tomorrow and on the shelves of the big box stores all up and down I-5," said Mckenzie, her voice raised to be heard over the rain.

"Great. It won't take me long. After that I'll get my supplies and come back and start painting."

"Wonderful. I've got a ton of things to do on the computer, so if you need me, I'll be in the front office."

"I think I'll be fine. I'll check in before I leave today."

Mckenzie walked off. Gina pulled her phone out of the small cross-body bag. She knelt down on the concrete and began taking photos. She had to move about five times to get good shots of all the small bulbs.

Then she went back to the fritillary greenhouse. Gina was alone. She took photos of the two different types of plants.

Then she returned to the first greenhouse. It took a bit longer because there were more different types of plants and she wanted to get all of them. By the time she finished, Gina had decided to paint one of the crown imperial fritillaries. They were stunning. She zipped her phone into the pocket of her fleece vest.

She went to Cory's office. He looked buried with paperwork. He glanced up when she came in the door.

"Just getting my supply bag," said Gina.

"Welcome to the team," he grinned, then looked back at the pile of papers.

Gina returned to the greenhouse. She set up the easel on a side walkway, hoping it was out of the way. Then got out her watercolor block and poured some water from her drinking water bottle into a small plastic container. Pulled out the brushes and watercolor palette.

She laid down a wash of a very pale-green background. Then lay it flat on the concrete to dry a little. Half of watercolor painting seemed to be standing around waiting for paint to dry. Too short and you'd mess things up. Too long and you'd mess things up.

Angie was in the next greenhouse, bent over and looking at plants. Then, before Gina could open her mouth, the entire line of hanging baskets was falling.

They hit the ground before she could cry out. Her voice deafened by the sound of wood baskets falling. The rain pounded on the greenhouse roofs.

Angie lay beneath the wood baskets.

"Help!" Gina yelled, through the open door nearest her.

Then hurried to the other greenhouse. Angie lay unmoving.

Gina began pulling the baskets off Angie. The hooks on the end kept getting tangled up in the line.

By the time she'd gotten Angie cleared, other people had arrived. Two of them were men whose names she didn't know.

Then Sarah came. She tried to open Angie's eyes. Angie didn't respond.

The concrete was wet with blood. There was no way this wasn't going to require medical care.

Gina pulled out her cell and called 911.

One of the men had run to get Cory. Soon there was a crowd around Angie. Gina stepped back out of the way.

Cory sat on the ground cradling Angie's head in his hands. And crying. Angie still breathed, but hadn't opened her eyes.

Gina stood at the back of the crowd, stunned. She couldn't focus on anything, overwhelmed with emotion. This was just simply awful.

By the time the ambulance people arrived with a stretcher, people had cleared away all the hanging baskets to make a path. The EMTs examined her and quickly conferred with Cory while everyone else stood around listening to the rain.

Gina looked at the faces surrounding her and saw the shock and horror that Angie had been nearly killed. Only a day after Dustin's murder.

The EMTs rolled the stretcher out.

Cory said, "I'm going to the hospital in the ambulance. Jason follow me in my car."

Cory tossed Jason his keys. The older man caught them and headed to the parking lot.

Cory said to everyone there, "They think Angie's going to be all right, but it's a bad head injury. Don't touch anything else in this greenhouse, just go on with your day as best you can and leave this greenhouse alone. The police are on their way and will want to see everything, just in case this wasn't an accident. I'll call from the hospital and give the office an update."

Cory ran after the stretcher.

Gina felt relieved the police were coming. It was too near Dustin's death to believe this was an accident. Angie could have been killed. But why would anyone want to kill her? She'd seemed well-liked.

"Okay everybody move along. I'll close both the doors," said one of the workers, whose name Gina didn't know.

The man closed the outside door and then after everyone had left, closed the one closest to the greenhouse Gina had been working in. She went to her watercolor block.

The wash was completely dry now. Wouldn't work at all for what she'd planned. She'd just use it as a preliminary painting to loosen up a bit.

Mckenzie came over to her and asked, "Do you think it was intentional?"

Everyone else had gone towards the main shipping area.

"I don't know. I'm not comfortable thinking it's an accident, not so soon after Dustin. But I don't know how that line works. Has it ever broken before?"

"Not that I know of. It's only three years old and I've never heard of any problems with it. Ever."

"Who maintains it?"

"Usually Jason adjusts the fertilizer levels. But we have a mechanic on site who keeps the motor humming along. I guess I should call him, huh? The police will want to talk to him about it."

"I'm sure they will," said Gina.

"And you didn't see anyone?" asked Mckenzie.

"No one was in that greenhouse, except Angie, when the baskets fell."

But there had been that man in there earlier, adjusting something with the water lines. Gina didn't know his name. She'd need to find out.

"I should talk to the police when they get here. I saw the baskets fall and I was the first to get to her. I don't know what I can tell them, but it might be something," said Gina.

Mckenzie nodded.

"But it's afternoon. If I don't eat now, I won't get another chance for hours. Questioning always takes a long time," said Gina.

"Go eat then," said Mckenzie. "I'll tell them you're in the break room, ready to talk to them after you eat. You can leave all your painting stuff right here. No one will bother it. I'm not sure much work's going to get done today."

Gina nodded. She picked up the watercolor block, set it on the easel and moved it next to the greenhouse wall. Then dug through her supplies for the lunch bag. She pushed the rest of her things against the wall. Then picked up the lunch bag and water bottle.

She and Mckenzie walked to the shipping room. The police had just driven up, the black SUV parked behind a semi being loaded with plants.

"Go quick, while you can," said Mckenzie.

GINA RUSHED TO THE BREAK ROOM. SHE SAT AT A TABLE NEAR Sarah and a young woman she recognized from the office, who was introduced as Emily.

"This is horrible," said Sarah.

Gina nodded. Would she even be able to eat?

She had to or her blood sugar would drop and she'd end up shaking. She opened the container with her sandwich. As soon as she smelled the tuna, her stomach began growling. She crunched down on a dill pickle chunk. The food tasted wonderful. Gina hadn't realized how hungry she'd been.

"Do you think it was an accident?" asked Emily.

"I don't believe in accidents," said Sarah. "And especially not after Dustin's death. Jason said that since Bob retired last fall, everything's been going downhill. His kids aren't spending money on maintenance."

"Do you believe him?" asked Emily.

"I don't know. But he's been here the longest. He would know."

"I heard he's angry because he was expecting to get Cory's job." Emily sipped from her cup of coffee.

"That's just silly," said Sarah. "Everybody knew Bob was gonna tap his kids for the top jobs in the company."

"Maybe not everybody."

"Maybe not," said Sarah. "I knew. Both Cory and Angie deserved their jobs. Dustin I'm not so sure, but there wasn't any competition for his job. Nobody here wanted to do marketing. Or knew anything about it. Except Mckenzie and I can't picture her as being behind a murder."

Gina swallowed and asked, "Did she want Dustin's job?"

"No, but she does know a lot about marketing and people and things. And she'll do a better job than Dustin did. He was just creepy," said Emily, dramatically shivering.

Sarah nodded.

Gina sipped some water and then launched into the other half of her sandwich.

"You're eating like a starving person," said Sarah.

"The police just arrived. And I saw the baskets come down and was the first person there. I know they'll want to talk to me. I'm trying to cram my lunch in fast," said Gina.

Another group of people came into the break room. One of them was the man who had been working with the water lines.

"I know so few people here," said Gina. "Could you start telling me people's names? Like that group who just sat down. With some repetition I might remember people."

"Okay the green hat, that's Juan. The blue shirt, Trang. The blue shirt with longer hair, Eric. The older guy with the stubble, David. The woman, Jessica. They work in the field mostly. Taking care of the perennials.

Trang. That was his name.

Gina finished her sandwich, sipped some water and got up.

"You haven't even taken a half hour lunch," said Sarah.

"I'm not on the clock. And I haven't worked a half day either," said Gina. "But thank you for looking out for me, that's very sweet. Believe me, I'll rest if I need it. I haven't made it to my age by skipping breaks."

Gina went out to the greenhouse where her art supplies were. The police were in the other greenhouse, four of them.

Gina recognized Deputy Hammond and Deputy Hofsteader. A tall black woman, with short hair that had gray in it, stood talking to Mckenzie. Another young officer, who she recognized from the other day, was also there.

She set her lunch bag and water bottle down. Then went towards the other greenhouse. She opened the sliding door a bit. When the tall woman stopped talking, Gina got Mckenzie's attention.

"I'm back from lunch. I'll be next door until you need me."

"Oh Gina, come in. The Sheriff was just asking about you."

Gina came in and closed the door.

"I"ll call you if I need you, Ms., ..." said the Sheriff.

"Fisher. Mckenzie Fisher. But really, call me Mckenzie. Nobody knows my last name around here. It's a casual place to work."

McKenzie went out the door.

"I'm Gina Wetherby," she said, holding out her hand to shake. "You must be Sheriff Winters."

"And you witnessed the accident."

"I was just next door. I looked up and saw all the baskets falling. They fell and hit Angie. She went down and they kept falling. I yelled for help and then ran to her. I pulled as many baskets off as I could, trying to uncover her. By then other people had come in."

"And you called 911?"

"I did. I saw blood on the concrete from her head and she still wasn't moving. It takes so long for medical help, we're so far away out here on the Island. I thought it was wise to call."

"It was. The Dr. said she'll recover, but it will take time. She's got a bad concussion. They're not sure about other injuries yet."

"Good."

"And what do you do here?" asked Sheriff Winters.

"I've been hired to paint plants for labels and plant tags."

"I thought this was their busy time. Shouldn't those be done already?"

"They're for next year."

"Ah. So you're a contractor?"

"I guess I am. I do botanical art. Mostly I just paint and people buy my paintings. This is the first time I've been hired to work like this."

"How long have you been working here?"

"Today's my first real day."

"But you were here on Tuesday?"

"I was. I came to see if I wanted to take the job. Sheriff Jansson encouraged me to accept it. And keep my eyes open."

Should she have said that? She didn't know if the two sheriffs had a good working relationship.

"And what have you seen?"

"I'm not sure. There was a man working on the water lines down there, this morning. At least that's what it looked like. He was on a lift, tinkering with something. His name is Trang. I don't know if it's connected to the accident. When I came back through later, he'd moved on to another job somewhere else."

"Is he still here?"

"In the break room when I left it. I also heard, and this is just rumor, that not everyone is happy with management. Bob Taylor, the founder, retired last year. It sounds like he gave his kids, Cory, Angie and Dustin, the top management positions. And overlooked some people in the process. I don't know if there's any truth to that. I just overhead it. That's all I know for now."

"We'll be looking into it. Well, thank you, Ms. Wetherby," said Sheriff Winters, crisply.

"You're welcome."

Gina turned and left the greenhouse, feeling dismissed. The Sheriff may or may not have believed her. She certainly was cool and didn't give a hint of what was going on within. Not someone you'd want to play poker with.

Gina left the greenhouse where Angie had been injured, sliding the door closed behind her. She felt relieved Angie would recover and hoped it would be swift.

This was their busy season. If the plants didn't go out, or if they were substandard, Taylor Gardens' reputation, and the business, would certainly suffer.

She looked at the blank wash on her easel. She'd need to hurry and get to painting. These plants might be gone by the time she got here tomorrow morning.

Gina tore the front page off the pad and set it aside. She'd use it later for something else. She moved her easel back to the center of the side aisle and pulled out the pot she wanted to paint, setting the plant in front of her.

And began again.

She was halfway through the painting when a team of workers came in and began moving the plants in the other half of the room. They loaded up plants into plastic crates, like those she'd seen yesterday. Then a machine picked up the pallet and took it out to the shipping room, setting it on the conveyor belt.

It was steady work with lots of bending. All of the workers were younger, probably in their twenties. Gina couldn't have done that, not for hours on end. It took the six of them, working steadily, a little over two hours to empty half of the greenhouse.

She finished two paintings of the crown fritillaries before they came to work on her half of the greenhouse. The head of the team introduced herself as Shawna.

"Oh, that's beautiful," she said, looking at the painting.

"Thank you. They're interesting plants."

"We can work on the other side if you want to do more."

"I'm fine. I think I'll work on another plant. I'll go to the greenhouse with the crocus and grape hyacinths. If they're still there."

"We'll be working on those after we've emptied this greenhouse," said Shawna.

"You're fast. So I've got about two hours."

"Well, probably longer. I don't think we'll get to it by quitting time. But we will, first thing tomorrow morning."

"What time do you stop?"

"Three-thirty. Unless someone allows us to work overtime."

"Allows you?"

"Yes. When Cory came in, he changed the rules to make them more fair to workers. Bob had been using Agricultural labor laws, which are looser. We work forty hour weeks and any overtime we work is paid time and a half. Cory has cut the amount of mandatory overtime. I think he and Angie have been better at planning than Bob was by himself. There isn't as much overtime, but there's more breaks and the few of us who are employed year round get vacation time and paid health insurance."

Gina nodded. Her friend Melanie had complained often about the lack of benefits nurseries provided. It was hard physical work and most often, seasonal employment. Many of the workers were immigrants. Melanie had worked at more than one place where the owners had taken advantage of those employees' ignorance of state laws or inability to speak English.

Ravenswood Nursery, even though small, had bucked the tide and been fair to their employees. Which kept good employees returning year after year, along with their expertise.

Many business owners simply didn't value their employees enough. Nurseries were no exception.

"So is everybody better off with Cory in charge?" asked Gina.

"The permanent workers are. The seasonal workers are, I think, but not as much as those of us who are here year round. I know Cory's raised wages across the board. He's much more hands on than Bob was and people trust him. Those of us who have been here for a while, worked side by side with Cory."

"How long have you been here?" asked Gina.

"Six years."

"And you'll be here next year?"

"I don't know. I'm not sure where my life's going right now. I'm pregnant."

"Oh, congratulations. When are you due?"

"Not till September. I'm so excited."

"Is this your first?"

"Yes."

"You're in for an exciting adventure."

"I'm ready for it. Or as ready as I will be. I'd better get back to work."

Gina nodded and said, "Me too. It was nice chatting with you."

Shawna returned to pulling plants to ship.

Gina picked up her watercolor block, tucking the finished dried paintings inside. Then put it into her bag. She collapsed the easel and stuck it in too. Plus the paints and brushes.

She'd have to walk outside to get to the other greenhouse, since the police were still in the adjoining one.

It was raining outside, so she put her hat and raincoat on and picked everything up. Gina went out the door at the far end farthest from the office. She carried the container of muddy-colored paint water and once outside, dumped it on the gravel.

Circling around the greenhouses was a wide concrete driveway, probably so the semis didn't have to turn around. Beyond that lay the growing fields. She could tell some plants were in the ground, but many were in black pots. Some were being carefully inspected and loaded up into crates by several workers.

Gina walked to the greenhouse and went inside. It was just slightly warmer than the temperature outside. She took her hat and coat off, leaving them on the floor next to the greenhouse wall. What should she work on first?

There were four varieties of *Iris reticulata*. The usual purple, a pinky-plum color, a yellow and a delicate blue with white and yellow.

Gina decided to work on that one. She set up her easel off to the side and refilled the water container from her water bottle, remembering to drink some of the clean water herself. Part of her resolution to drink more water.

She pulled one of the pots out from its row and examined it. *Iris reticulata 'Katharine Hodgkin'*. In pencil, she wrote the name on the bottom of the next clean piece of paper on the watercolor block.

She'd forgotten to write the fritillary's name, but had taken photos of all the current plant tags, so she'd do that later.

She pulled her paints and brushes out and began mixing paint for a wash. Most of the petals were white, so she'd do a gray wash.

In the middle greenhouse, the police were down at the far end, where the line had broken.

They'd had a two-person lift brought in and Sheriff Winters and a worker Gina hadn't seen before were up on it, examining the line. The man seemed to be talking. He was pointing to a piece of the line above them and shaking his head.

Gina continued to paint, while watching the police. She didn't know what they'd found. But photos were taken and the worker was interviewed for a very long time. He looked uncomfortable. Sheriff Winters was formidable.

Gina's phone buzzed. She pulled it out of the side pocket of her vest.

"Hello," she said.

"Are you causing trouble again?" asked Melanie.

"Doing my best. Why?"

"I just heard about Dustin Taylor. And that his sister's in the hospital. What happened."

Gina quickly talked about Dustin's murder and Angie's injury."

"My goodness. Are Cory and Bob worried?"

"I haven't seen Bob since Dustin was killed. I think he's at home. And Cory's at the hospital with Angie. Where'd you hear about the problems?"

"Karen told me. She heard it from someone down at Corr's."

Karen was the current owner of Ravenswood Nursery.

"Ah Corr's. The source of all local gossip. How much cake did she buy?"

The grocery store sold full and half cakes.

"Only half. It's Terry's birthday. And all of us are either dieting or not eating carbs. Except for our two young male minions. Who could eat an entire cake each, I'm sure."

"What else did you hear?"

"Dustin's funeral is Saturday. Are you going?"

"I suppose I should. I didn't know him, but I've known Bob for years."

"Me too. Let's go together. I hate funerals."

"Done."

"Where are you now?"

"I'm at Taylor Gardens. Painting."

"What?"

"I just did a crown fritillary. Now I'm working on a pretty blue. white and yellow *Iris reticulata*."

"'*Katharine Hodgkin*'?"

"Yes. I think that's the name."

"I love that one. I should go out and check if mine at home are blooming yet. Probably not, if Taylor's is just shipping them."

"This greenhouse isn't very warm. But they are shipping the rest out tomorrow. I think they're a day behind."

"Well, I better get back to work. And you better get to painting before those plants walk out the door."

"Great. I'll come pick you up on Saturday. Let me know what time," said Gina.

"Will do. TTFN."

Gina tucked the phone back into her vest and zipped up the pocket. Melanie was spending too much time with her grandbabies. TTFN. She vaguely remembered Tigger saying that. *Ta-Ta For Now.*

She put the final details into the painting. There. It was quite lovely and captured the flower nicely.

Gina also did a painting of the pinky-plum one as well. The markings on that *Iris* weren't as complex as the blue one, but it would make a pretty splash of spring color in the garden.

She glanced at her phone to check the time. It was past 3:30. Most of the workers would have left then. She'd been here for more than six hours. Her feet and knees hurt, despite wearing her cushy running shoes. Standing on concrete all day wasn't good.

Gina decided to go home and do a couple more paintings tonight. Sitting down. She packed everything up. The police were gone, but it wasn't clear they were done in the next greenhouse. She put on her raincoat and hat.

Then went out the door at the far end and walked across

the courtyard to the office. She found a gravel area to dump her paint water. She went into the main shipping area. It was empty, but Cory's door was open and the light in his office was on.

Gina poked her head in and saw Cory at his desk, typing on the keyboard.

"I'm on my way out. Is there any news on Angie?"

"Oh hi Gina. Helluva day, huh? She's conscious, but they said it'll take days to find the extent of her injuries."

"Oh dear. I'm glad to hear she's awake. But that must really hurt, losing one of your managers."

"Frankly, I don't know how we're going to pull this season off. I'll need to hire someone who's skilled and knowledgeable about plants, production, natural pest management, oh and good at working with others. In the middle of the season. When anyone who's even adequate already has a job. There's no one here who has Angie's skillset. She's a gem and I'm not saying that just because she's my sister."

"So you're putting out a call for a manager?"

"I am. Several. I hope I find someone good, and fast, who'll take the job for a short time. Might be the full season, or might be longer. The docs can't tell me when Angie might be back. And she can barely speak, so she can't tell me either."

"That must be really frustrating," said Gina.

"Sorry, I didn't mean to unload on you. Cass, my wife, has got her hands full, taking care of Dad and wrangling our youngest. Who's in her last year of high school and dealing with graduation coming up and starting college in the fall. I haven't told Cass about Angie yet. I will when I get home."

"How's Bill doing?"

"He's staying with us right now. He took Dustin's murder

hard. As did we all. And the attack on Angie ... well I don't know how he'll take that. That's why I wanted to wait till I got home to tell him and Cass. Hoping maybe the police can tell us it was all an accident."

"Does it seem like an accident to you?"

"No. That line has never broken. Ever. The motors have gone down. The waterline's have gotten plugged. But the line for the plants has always been solid. And they were all inspected two months ago. Thoroughly."

"Oh dear," said Gina.

"You haven't heard anything, have you? I know you were working just next door while the police were there."

"No. I spoke to Sheriff Winters, but she wasn't giving anything away. Just asking questions."

Cory rubbed his face.

"Well, I guess they'll tell us when they know something."

"I'll let you finish up. I need to go sit down and put my feet up."

"Standing on concrete sure makes your feet hurt. It does make things easier to clean up though."

"Your greenhouses are immaculate."

"Well, it keeps the pests down."

"I'll see you tomorrow," said Gina.

"I'll most likely be here. I'll try to get to the hospital in the early morning. Then come here."

Gina went through the office, but Mckenzie wasn't there. Gina signed out on the visitors' clipboard and waved at Emily, who was working at a computer.

It was still raining outside as she clumsily slid into her car. Her legs felt relieved to sit down. Maybe she should have taken more breaks today. Tomorrow, she'd bring her camp chair and sit down between paintings.

She drove home by way of Corr's, to pick up half a roasted chicken, some coleslaw and half a chocolate cake. There was no way she was cooking tonight.

GINA PARKED IN HER SMALL GARAGE AND CLOSED THE LARGE door. The garage was new, from last summer. She'd had builders remove the dilapidated carport and build a garage. It made her feel a bit safer from the winds that whipped off Puget Sound and through the neighborhood. Another year and the carport would probably have fallen on its own.

It would take two trips into the house to bring everything in, but she needed to wash the brushes and remove the finished paintings.

She took the groceries in first and was greeted with complaints from her Maine Coon cats.

"Oh you two, it's an hour till dinner time. I've gotten home in plenty of time to feed you."

Albert wrapped himself around her legs and Alice, an orange and white streak, shot through the open door to explore the garage. Gina set the cloth grocery bag on the counter. She removed the cake and set it on the counter. Then the chicken, putting it on the stove. And the coleslaw, debating for a minute whether to put it into the fridge. No, she'd eat soon, then refrigerate the rest.

She hung up her rain hat and coat in the tiled area between the front door and the garage. Back out in the garage, she opened the car door and pulled out her art supplies, then quickly closed the door before Alice could get in.

That cat adored exploring new territory and was sniffing the wheels. What did she smell? The road mud from the parking lot of Corr's? Or of Taylor's? Whatever it was, she was fascinated.

Albert only had one item on his agenda. He sat near the bowl of clean water, waiting for his food bowl to be set down.

Gina went to her studio, opened the door, closing it behind her to keep the cats out and set the art supply bag on the floor. She pulled everything out. Then got the finished paintings out of the watercolor pad, laying them on her empty worktable. She pulled the dirty brushes out as well as the water container and took them to the studio sink to wash out and lay on a clean rag to dry.

Then went to her bedroom and sat on the chair by the closet, taking her shoes off. She slipped into a pair of comfy wool clogs. Her feet felt relieved.

Tonight would be a good night for a glass of wine. She had some chilling in the fridge. By the time Gina returned to the kitchen, Alice was finished exploring and had joined Albert.

Gina ignored them and closed the garage door. Then she took the phone out of her pocket, checked for messages and plugged it in to recharge.

No mail had come in the door slot. There wouldn't be any packages outside, she wasn't expecting anything.

Gina looked at the clock. It was 4:30 p.m. The cats wouldn't allow her to eat in peace. So she opened a can of their grain-free food and fed them. Even if it was early.

She opened the bottle of Sauvignon blanc and poured a glass. Then put some of the roasted chicken on a plate and stuck it in the microwave. Her stomach growled hungrily as she sipped the wine.

This one tasted slightly oaky, which she appreciated. It had the crisp fruitiness good Washington wines were known for.

The microwave pinged and the doorbell rang at the same time. Gina sighed and went to the front door. The cats were still eating.

She looked through the peephole. Sheriff Jannson. Probably here in his official capacity.

She opened the door and said, "Come on in."

"I can't stay."

"Cats. Come on in."

He nodded and rushed in the door. She closed it behind him.

"I'm just here to get your view of what happened today."

"Well, wipe your feet and come in. My dinner's ready and I need to sit down. You're welcome to join me."

He followed her into the kitchen. The cats barely looked up, they were used to his comings and goings.

Gina took her steaming plate out of the microwave with a potholder and added some coleslaw to it.

"Nothing fancy, I wasn't in the mood to cook tonight."

"I don't blame you. I just ate though."

She nodded and took her wine and plate over to the table. She sat down and he pulled up another chair.

She took a bite of the coleslaw. Crunchy cabbage,

complemented with a tangy vinegar mayonnaise sauce and the bite of caraway seeds.

"I heard what happened through Detective Hofsteader. I wanted to know what you had to say."

"Well, I reported most of what I know to Sheriff Winters. Afterwards I talked to a couple of people. One of the workers said that Cory changed things when he took over. Made the working conditions better, increased wages, that sort of thing. There was less mandatory overtime. She seemed to think it was the combination of Cory and Angie working together. Both of them had spent more time working in the greenhouses than Bob did. I spoke to Cory before I left. He's in a bad way. Worried about Angie, his dad, his family. And the business. He has to hire someone to replace Angie at the peak of the season. And Angie's got unusual skills. So, he's frustrated. I expect he's afraid too. He doesn't think her injury was an accident. The lines were inspected two months ago. They've never broken. So Angie's been severely injured, no one knows how serious it is yet, but she's probably out for the rest of the busy season at least."

She took a deep breath and ate a bite of the roast chicken. It was still moist and full of flavor.

"I don't believe in coincidences. I think someone tried to kill Angie. I'm not sure why. I can only think that they're trying for the entire family. That this is either about the business, or a way to get back at Bob for something. I don't have a clear motive or a clear suspect," he said.

Gina sipped more of the wine.

"But you've got some suspects?"

"Several."

"Whose investigation is this? Are you working with Sheriff Winters?"

"Because she's replacing me, we're sharing information, but each running our own investigation."

"That must put the deputies in a strange spot."

"Deputy Hammond is assisting me, Hofsteader's helping Winters. So is Carstears. Beales is helping me. It's complicated, but the Sheriff wanted this. She wanted the chance to prove herself, with backup."

"But Deputy Hammond was helping her this afternoon."

"Yes, we're shorthanded. Hammond can't report to Winters though. That's been made clear."

"So, this is sort of like a contest? See who solves the case first?"

"Not exactly," he said, grinning. "Although I'm giving her an edge. I want her to succeed or else I'll never get to retire. It's more her doing the job, me shadowing her and stepping in if there's a problem or if she's missing something big. She's lacking in local knowledge and a little in confidence."

"I'm happy to be in neither of your shoes."

"It's not the best, but she's new and although I trust that she was a good cop in Chicago, I'm not sure she'll work out here. She has an abruptness that won't let people trust and confide in her. Not the officers she's working with or the people she's interviewing."

"I can see that," said Gina. "Care to enlighten me on who your main suspects are? So I can see if anyone at Taylor Gardens opens up about them?"

"You know I can't do that."

"Okay. I understand. Can you tell me if I should

concentrate on schmoozing with the office people or the other workers?"

He raised an eyebrow at her.

"Okay, no hints. I'll just have to talk to everyone. Don't know how I'm going to have time to get all these paintings done with all that talking."

"There's a lot to do?"

Gina unzipped her left vest pocket and pulled out the folded up plant lists that Mckenzie had printed out earlier in the day. She unfolded it and handed it to him.

He looked at it and said, "You need to do a painting for each one?"

"Those are just the ones for the next month. She didn't want to print out farther than that, just in case things go badly off schedule. Which under the circumstances is pretty smart."

The Sheriff whistled and handed the list back to her.

"I think each of us would prefer our own jobs to the others. Then again, I'd prefer no job right now."

"Why did you decide to retire so quickly."

"I've been thinking about it for years. But lately, especially after we met for coffee or tea, I decided that if I wasn't going to ruin this possible relationship, like I did my marriage, then it was time to retire. I know there are cops who can have both a relationship and the job. I'm not one of them."

He stopped talking and looked at her, obviously waiting until what he said could sink in.

Gina took a deep breath.

"I know you said you weren't ready for commitment. I'm not either. Yet. But I will be after I can convince you I'm a worthwhile companion," he said.

"I think you've already convinced me of that," she said. "I

just don't know if you're the right one for me. Like I said, I want to move slowly on this."

"How slowly?" he asked.

"Well, although I've known you for a couple of years, as the Sheriff, but I'd like to know you on a dating level for a couple of months before I leap into anything," she said. "We've only had one date."

"That sounds just fine to me. I don't think I'll be any good at dating while I've got this job. If there's a case, I'm like a terrier. I just can't seem to let it go."

"I understand that."

"And this case is bad. One of the reasons I won't share information with you, besides the legal and ethical ones, is that I want you to drop the job with Taylor Gardens. I should never have encouraged you to take it. I wasn't thinking straight. I think it's a very dangerous place to be right now. I think someone's targeting the Taylors, yes, but there might be fallout. I don't want you in danger. There, I've said it. I don't expect that you'll quit. I know you better than that. But I had to say it."

"Thank you for your honesty. You're right, I can't quit. But I'll be very careful."

Albert jumped up on his lap at that moment and stood there, waiting to be petted.

The Sheriff laughed and petted the cat.

"Decided I was okay, huh?"

Albert meowed in response. And began purring as the Sheriff stroked his long fur.

"You're going to regret that," Gina said. "At least his fur is black and gray. Might blend better with black uniform.

"Not the worst thing I've had stuck to my uniform," he said.

Alice was sitting in the window, gazing out at the garden and watching the new leaves on trees blow in the wind.

"Are we expecting a storm?"

"I haven't heard," he said.

"Why did Sheriff Winters come all the way across the country for a job?"

"She has a teenage son who was being bullied. She's a single mom and decided a complete change of scene would help him. I hope it does"

"I hope it helps too. I've heard the local schools have a strong stance against bullying, but I'm sure it still happens. It must be hard being a single mom who's got such a demanding job. Does she know anyone out here?"

"Not that I know of. I'm guessing she'd just had enough and applied for a lot of jobs, then jumped at the first offer that came her way. She must have taken a pay cut to come here and housing's more expensive in this area than Chicago. It must have been a tough choice. We haven't talked about that. Just the job. She's very closed-mouthed."

"I got that impression. I told her you'd asked me to keep my eyes and ears open. I couldn't tell what she thought about that."

"I couldn't tell you either. She's very smart, strong and has a good record. I think she'll do fine, but she'll need to learn to open up a little in order to gain the trust of the other officers. It'll take some time. Well, I'd better get back to work. I just wanted to make sure you're all right."

"I'm fine. I was really shaken up this morning. I saw the accident happen. I was so afraid for Angie."

"I want you to be very careful. And spend as little time around Cory as you can. I don't want you to get hurt."

"I'll see what I can do," said Gina. "Wait, you don't think he's a suspect?"

"No. I just think he'll be the next target. Or maybe they'll go for Bob. I don't know and it frustrates me."

Gina nodded.

He set Albert down on the floor and Gina walked him to the front door.

"I hope the next time I see you, I'm unemployed," said the Sheriff.

"That would be nice. But don't stay away just because you're not."

She let him out the door and locked it after he left.

Then returned to her dinner. The chicken was cold, but still tasted good. The cake was even better, rich and chocolatey.

After she'd cleaned up the dirty dishes, Gina went to her studio. She set up some good watercolor paper on the permanent easel and filled the water container that lived there. Gathered all her brushes and paint.

Then she unplugged and opened up the iPad to her photos. The new ones from today were already there. She chose one to work on, the grape hyacinth.

Gina pulled up her tall stool with the back and sat on it while she painted. Her sore feet and knees appreciated sitting.

Two paintings took about an hour. She should keep track of her time as well as the number of paintings. That would help her to decide if she needed to renegotiate the contract.

She washed up the brushes and decided to call it a night. It would be good to get to bed earlier tonight and do a lot more painting on site tomorrow.

Gina repacked her supply bag, except for the wet brushes. She would stick them in tomorrow morning.

Then she went out to the garage and put her camp chair in the car. Alice didn't follow her this time. Both cats were snoozing on the couch.

She sat down on the couch between them, petting one with each hand, her feet on the coffee table. Thinking back on what the Sheriff, Bryan, had said. That he was serious enough about her to quit his job. Which she'd known he was weary of doing last year. But he was serious enough now to talk about it publicly. To put in notice, so the position would be advertised and a replacement found.

The thought made her smile. She really did like him and thought they could make a life together.

FRIDAY MORNING

THE NEXT MORNING GINA ARRIVED AT TAYLOR GARDENS BY eight. An hour earlier than yesterday. The sun was out this morning, but there were clouds on the horizon so the good weather might not last.

She signed in at the front desk. Mckenzie wasn't in the office.

According to her list, bleeding hearts, *Anemone nemorosa*, wallflowers and the first wave of *Calibrochoa* annual baskets were going out next. Gina had seen the *Calibrochoa* hanging in one of the greenhouses. She couldn't remember which one. She'd have to hunt all the plants down and find someone to lower a few of the hanging baskets for her to photograph.

Gina decided to take everything with her during the search and leave them in the first place she found plants on the list. Then continue her search for the others. Do the photographing first, painting second. She wouldn't be anywhere near Cory's office and wouldn't have to walk as far.

She found the bleeding hearts first. There were white, pink

and red varieties of *Dicentra spectabilis*. As well as the yellow-leafed variety which had been all the rage for a decade now. There was one in her own garden and Gina adored it. She should take a walk in her own small garden today and see if it was coming up yet.

The greenhouse was otherwise empty, so she set up her chair, putting it next to the wall and lay her supply bag on it. Then she went off looking for the other plants.

The greenhouse she'd been painting Iris in yesterday, was empty of all those plants. One end was being filled with new pots of all sorts of *Begonia* with dramatic-looking leaves. There were plum colored, green and silvery leaves, some swirled, others jagged and a few swirled around on top of themselves. She looked forward to painting the *Begonia*.

Gina tracked down the other plants. Taking photos of them when she found each group of plants, Gina saved the hanging baskets for last.

She found Jason supervising a group of workers loading new plants into an empty greenhouse.

"Jason, I don't know who to ask, but you might. I need a few of those hanging baskets down so I can photograph them in order to paint them. It won't take long, but they're going out this week or next." She pointed to the next greenhouse.

"I can do that for you," he said, with a charming smile that was almost too polite.

Jason said something to the workers, in Spanish.

Then he said, to Gina, "I'll need to get a lift. I'll meet you over there and you can tell me which baskets you need."

Gina nodded and returned to the greenhouse. From what she could see the baskets contained three different color combinations. She'd need one of each.

Jason returned a few minutes later driving the lift.

Gina pointed to the first one and he parked beneath it. He raised the lift and when he could reach the line, asked, "This one?"

"If it looks good to you. From down here it looks like there's three different color combinations. I need a good example of each one."

Jason looked at several others and chose one, then handed it down to her. He moved the machine a few feet down the line to get another one.

Gina set the pale pink and white-flowered basket in the center walkway and followed the machine. He handed her a yellow and pale orange-flowered basket, which she set near the first one. Then he got two more. One with yellow and white flowers and another that had purple and hot pink blooms. He lowered the lift and handed them over.

"Looks like there's four different color combos. You can just leave them in a row by the lift and I'll come back later and hang them up again."

"Thank you so much," she said.

"My pleasure. Everyone's really excited about you being here, you know."

"I didn't know."

"It's an honor to have an artist here painting our plants."

"Well thank you. There are some breathtaking plants here. It's fun to paint them."

He nodded and said, "Well, I better get back to my team. Make sure things are getting done right."

He walked off into another greenhouse. Leaving Gina to ponder relationships between coworkers.

Had Angie gotten along with everyone? She was younger

and apparently very skilled, but Jason was in his fifties, Gina guessed. He'd been at the company longer and at least had experience, if not knowledge. Along came the boss' kids to take over management. Had he even gotten a promotion? A pay raise?

Gina pondered how she could tactfully ask Cory or Mckenzie such a thing without raising suspicion. There really wasn't a way, unless it came up in conversation somehow.

And Sheriff Jannson had told her to stay away from Cory, just in case he was a target.

Maybe she could figure out a way to bring it up with Mckenzie. If she ever saw Mckenzie. Who must be terribly busy trying to do both her own job and Dustin's. Had she hired someone as an assistant yet? That position ought to be easier to fill than Angie's.

Gina took off her fleece jacket and wrapped it around her waist, leaving her vest on. Then took many photos of the *Calibrochoa*. This greenhouse was much warmer than the others. They were probably trying to give the annuals a boost so the baskets would look nice and full by the time they hit the stores.

She wasn't fond of buying annuals, preferring bulbs and perennials that came back year after year. But some annuals had a lot of zing and added something to the garden. Especially since they bloomed all summer nonstop. Few perennials did that.

Mostly, Gina liked annuals in containers, but she wasn't about to plant any herself. Too much dead-heading and watering. She didn't enjoy gardening that much. Painting was much more fun.

She enjoyed seeing them in other people's gardens though. Just like some other high-maintenance plants.

Gina wanted exotic-looking, but easy to care for plants. And she didn't have much room in her garden, so it was crammed full of those. She didn't have to venture into using plants that demanded more care.

Finishing up with the hanging baskets, she set them near the lift and returned to the greenhouse with her belongings. Gina set up her easel and decided to begin with the bleeding heart that had red and white flowers.

She walked along the rows and found several that were farther along than the others. Then chose one pot to paint.

The fluffy-lacy leaves of this variety had more of a bluish-green cast than the straight species. The arching stems were burgundy. From the stem hung red poofy hearts with a white spear-like protrusion from the end. There simply was nothing like seeing bleeding hearts in the spring to lift one's spirits.

Gina laid down a wash of pale-green paint and set it aside to dry for a few minutes. While she waited, Gina walked down the walkway and chose a *Dicentra spectabilis 'Goldheart'* to paint next. The chartreuse-colored foliage glowed and perfectly accented the bright pink and white flowers.

She was carrying it back to her easel when a loud noise blasted through the area. The sound was deafening.

Gina instantly squatted near to the ground, setting the plant down and covering her head with her arms. Was the greenhouse actually made of glass or plastic?

Nothing seemed to be falling, but she heard yelling over the ringing in her ears. That had been loud.

The earth around her had moved.

Earthquake? Explosion?

Two workers ran past her. A third, Shawna, stopped and helped Gina up.

"Are you all right?" asked Shawna, out of breath.

"Yes. What was that?"

"Gas explosion maybe, it sounded bad. Do you have a phone on you?"

"Yes."

"Call 911."

Then Shawna ran after the others, towards where the noise had come from.

Gina called 911 and stayed on the line while walking in the same direction. She'd been in the greenhouse adjoining the courtyard. Everyone seemed to be heading towards the shipping area. Towards Cory's office.

Where the most people would have been working, shipping and loading plants.

Gina made it into the greenhouse next to shipping. Black smoke billowed out from the next greenhouse, through the now open roof. There were shiny pieces of grit beneath her feet. It felt hard, like glass not plastic. The adjoining greenhouse walls were gone. All that remained were bent metal frames.

She couldn't go any farther. The pathways were all blocked with workers who couldn't go in because of all the smoke.

"I can't see," she told the 911 operator. "There's too much smoke. The glass has been blown out of the greenhouse frames. It's the shipping area on the northwest corner of the buildings."

"Can you see flames?"

"No, there's too much smoke."

"Fire and EMTs are on their way."

"Better call the Sheriff too. This isn't the first problem here this week," said Gina.

"Please, continue to stay on the line. Make sure you're in a safe place."

Gina looked up. The structure didn't feel safe to her.

She tapped the person in front of her on the shoulder.

"We should clear this greenhouse. I don't think it's safe. None of us can go forward anyway."

He nodded at her and began to talk to those around him. Everyone began to move rapidly to the surrounding greenhouses.

Gina did too. Should she go to the greenhouse she'd been working in and get her belongings?

There wasn't much of a choice as she was herded along with the pack of workers. She stuck her phone in her vest pocket and zipped it.

Then walked with the rest of them to the far end of the greenhouses and outside. It felt chilly out today. Gina had her jacket still wrapped around her waist. She untied it and slipped her arms in the sleeves, then zipped up.

She could hear the sirens now.

The group walked around to the front parking lot and saw two large firetrucks pull in. Then several ambulances and two police SUVs. They disappeared behind a semi parked in the loading area.

Gina followed the others over to that corner of the property. A column of black smoke still roiled up into the air. She couldn't see any flames.

The front corner looked like it had a huge hole in it. About where Cory's office was. She sure hoped he hadn't been in it and that nobody had been hurt.

But his office was right next to the shipping area. There would have been a lot of people working to fill orders.

Gina stood with the others out in the parking lot. A deputy she didn't recognize came to find out what happened. Shawna talked to him. He took her statement and told them all to wait there.

People were worried. A couple of middle-aged women, who Gina heard speaking Spanish, huddled together crying.

A helicopter flew overhead, then hovered. The side had some sort of logo on it, but Gina couldn't make it out. Probably a news channel.

The smoke began to wane a little. Another group of workers came around the far end of the building. From the same direction Gina and the others had come.

Upon seeing them in the parking lot, they began to run over to them. Many embraced each other. No one seemed to know the extent of the damage or injuries. After listening to their conversations a while, it turned out that they'd been working out in the fields behind the greenhouses.

Gina couldn't see the loading area from where they stood. She couldn't see the back end of the semi either.

Her phone rang. She pulled it out of her vest pocket.

"Hello," she said.

"You're all right," said Melanie.

"I am. Just scared."

Three different news vans pulled up in the parking lot.

"The explosion's all over the news. Someone's got a copter overhead."

"I'm out in the parking lot. Should I wave at them?"

"What happened?"

"I have no idea. I was in one of the far greenhouses, gathering plants to paint, when there was an explosion. People came running. I followed them to where the explosion was. We couldn't go in, way too much smoke to see anything. We were standing in the greenhouse next to the explosion, the glass was all blown out, when I realized the whole frame might come down and we should get out of all the greenhouses. So we did."

"Was anyone hurt?"

"I don't know, there's a semi blocking my view from here. A couple of the workers have walked over to the road on that side of the building, but they're not back yet."

"Well, I've gotta get back to work. But you keep yourself safe."

"I might call you later, if I need a ride home."

"What's wrong with your new car?"

"The car's fine. She's sitting here in the parking lot. But they might not let us back in the greenhouses. And that's where my keys are."

"And your lunch."

"And my lunch. Why does this horrible person plan all this around lunchtime. Ugh. I might give up eating, just no appetite."

"You can't afford to lose any weight. Call me if you need me to bring you something, or a ride home. My schedule's flexible."

"Thanks."

She slipped the phone back in her vest pocket and zipped it up.

She watched as a semi behind them, turned into the long circular driveway that wrapped around the greenhouses. The far end of which was blocked by another semi, firetrucks and other emergency vehicles.

Three men ran over, waving their hands. The driver saw them and stopped. They talked to the driver and then the semi managed to back out and get on the street. Then they closed the gate, so more trucks wouldn't attempt to go in.

The two workers came back from the road past the semi.

The taller one spoke in a heavily accented voice, "There's a huge hole in the other side of the building. It was during lunch break. Shipping area might have been deserted. Maybe. Back of that semi is all burned up. Ambulances being loaded with injured people."

The other one walked through the crowd and showed people photos he'd taken on his phone. About half of the wall was blown away. It didn't look like there was any glass left in that greenhouse. Gina couldn't see the interior well. It all looked black from roiling smoke. The ground around the greenhouse sparkled with glass. Three or four people were out there with brooms trying sweep it into piles. A crowd of workers stood outside away from the greenhouses and at the far end of the fire, aid and police vehicles.

Was it like windshield glass that broke into non-sharp pieces? Or would it cut car tires?

It might not matter. Even if it wasn't sharp, those sweeping might just feel a need to be useful somehow. Gina felt frustrated and useless.

Two more Raven Island Police Dept. Vehicles drove up and parked. The officers went to the loading dock area. Gina recognized Sheriff Winters as one of them. Her bearing was so tall and regal.

Gina went over to Shawna.

"Is it true that it happened during a lunch break? Would the shipping area be empty then?"

"It was during the first lunch. But the shipping area is hardly ever empty during the day. And I don't know what the break room looks like right now. I don't know. We can only hope."

Three officers were coming towards them. As they came closer, Gina recognized Sheriff Jannson and Deputy Hammond. The third officer, she'd seen, but didn't know his name.

As they came closer, the workers began to ask questions.

She could see the moment the Sheriff spotted her. His face dropped into a relieved expression.

When he was close enough, he held up a hand.

"There's been a gas explosion, far as we can tell. The Fire Department is still putting out the fire. It looks like it's gonna burn awhile. Some people were injured, but most of those injuries are minor. Those folks have been seen to. Some injuries will require a trip to the hospital. I don't have names right now. There's a woman down there, Emily, I think is her name. She's got a clipboard and is taking names. She'll come over here when she finishes over there. Are any of you injured?"

No one stepped forward.

"Good. I don't want any of you to step foot back inside the buildings or greenhouses until we've had the firefighters' okay. There's some fears that the glass will fall. Even some of the structures. So please stay far away from everything right now. This is a good spot to be and it's not raining. Do you have any questions I can answer?"

"Is Cory okay?" asked one of the workers.

"We haven't found Cory yet. It's not clear if he was even on site this morning."

"Was this an accident?" asked another.

"We don't know. The Fire Department will be investigating that. They might be calling in outsiders to make that determination."

"How long before we can get back inside?" asked Shawna. "We need to try to salvage plants and water them. And I'm sure there's shipments to get out."

"Well, nothing's going anywhere until that side of the building is cleared of emergency vehicles and that semi gets towed away. You can't see from here, but the back end is completely burned up. It's missing a few wheels. There's still a lot of toxic smoke in those greenhouses. It'll have to vent out, provided that system's still working. We'll get you in to take care of the plants as soon as we can. But right now, we're focused on getting the fire out and finding all the people we know were here. People first, plants second."

Shawna nodded.

"My deputies will begin taking your statements."

Gina put her arm around Shawna's shoulder and the young woman leaned into her. She looked pale, her face drawn.

"You look tired."

"It's long past lunch. I'm tired and starving."

"Do you have your car keys?"

She shook her head.

"Me neither," said Gina. Then to the crowd, "Does anyone have their car keys and wallet?"

Only one young man did.

Gina said, "Some of us need some food. And probably

water. Can you take a run to Corr's and pick up some of their sandwiches?"

"How many people want them?" he asked.

Twenty-two people raised their hands.

"I need one that's vegetarian," said one young man.

"Non-dairy," said another.

"I need one with their gluten-free bread," said a woman.

"Slow down," said the young man, who was taking notes on his phone.

"The folks on the other side might want some too," said Gina.

"I'll go ask, then call in an order," he said.

Gina thought maybe his name was David, but couldn't be sure.

"How do I pay for it?" he asked.

Shawna said, "Ask Emily. Taylors' might have an account there."

The man sprinted off to go ask the others.

There was a raised bed between the parking lot and the road. Gina took Shawna over there and they sat on the two-foot tall boulders that outlined the bed. Others joined them.

"I needed to sit down," said Gina.

"So did I. I'm not that far along, but my ankles swell," said Shawna.

A siren began to wail as an ambulance drove off.

Gina hoped Cory wasn't inside.

FRIDAY AFTERNOON

THEY CONTINUED TO WAIT OUT IN THE PARKING LOT. THE WIND picked up, but luckily, it wasn't raining. It was just a normal early-spring day. Gray and in the fifties.

Many of the workers were in t-shirts and jeans, used to working in warm greenhouses. Several had hoodies, they'd been working out in the field. All work had stopped for today.

Would there even be a tomorrow for this company? The shipping area was completely burnt out. At least one greenhouse had no glass in it. The metal structure may or may not be a total loss.

Gina heard a couple of the workers speculating that the explosion had something to do with the propane tanks. Or a gas line. No one seemed clear on the answer and the deputies and sheriff kept saying they didn't know, as they took statements from everyone.

Sheriff Jannson took her statement. He sat down on a rock near her and asked questions.

She hadn't really seen anything, so had nothing to tell him.

The Sheriff told Gina that Mckenzie wasn't on site this morning. She'd been scheduled to meet with a caterer for an event in June. Gina felt relieved.

"But wait, if she wasn't here, does that make her a suspect?"

Sheriff Jannson just looked at her with his right eyebrow arched.

"Sorry, I know you can't tell me that. And you've heard nothing from Cory?"

He shook his head.

Her mouth felt dry. It had been two hours since the blast.

A forest green SUV pulled into the parking lot.

"That's Cory's car," said Shawna.

Sure enough Cory got out. He went running towards the loading dock, but Deputy Hammond grabbed him and pulled him towards Sheriff Jannson.

"Let me go. I need to go see what happened," he said.

"Don't make me cuff you," said the Deputy, as she wrestled him to stillness. Gina hadn't realized how strong she was.

"No one is going anywhere near the fire," said the Sheriff.

"What happened? I heard on the news there was a gas explosion."

"We don't know yet. The Fire Department will be investigating, once the fire's out and it's safe."

"Was anyone hurt?"

"Some people were. Mostly minor injuries. A couple are on their way to the hospital."

"Was anyone killed?" Cory asked.

"We don't know yet. Now, I have questions. Where were you?"

"I stayed home this morning. The internet's better there and I had a Skype meeting with a wholesaler. I didn't want to be interrupted. After that, I was going to come in, but I went to the hospital. They called and told me Angie's awake.

"Thank goodness," said Shawna.

"I'll need the name and contact info for the person you were having a meeting with," said the Sheriff.

Was Cory a suspect?

Of course he was. Anyone who owned a business that had the problems this one had recently would be. Especially since he hadn't been here this morning.

"Sure," said Cory. "I can get it for you. It's on my laptop. I left it in the car."

"I'll follow you," said Deputy Hammond.

But if Cory was going to blow up his own business, wouldn't he have done it at night? When no one was there? Gina had seen him as a person who cared about his workers.

Or perhaps he had and everything was going south. An explosion like that, if it was a gas leak, would probably be a tricky thing to time right.

"And you," said Sheriff Jannson, "can just go back to your painting."

"I can't," she said. "My supplies are in the greenhouse."

"You know what I mean."

"I have no intention of investigating a gas leak. I would like to know how Angie's doing though."

"I'm sure they don't know yet," he said. "Not if she just woke up."

"You're probably right," she said, grudgingly. But she wanted information. Good news about something. They all did.

Gina understood what was behind his ridiculous demand. He was feeling worried about her safety. Still it annoyed her.

"We'll let you folks know when you can get back inside and retrieve your belongings," said Sheriff Jannson. "If you'll all wait here until then."

The Sheriff and the other deputy followed Deputy Hammond and Cory. Eventually all four of them went around the front of the disabled semi and disappeared from sight.

David drove up in his small blue car. A group of people went over to get their food, or perhaps help him distribute it.

Gina stayed where she was, as did several others. After while, two young men came around with paper bags of sandwiches. Gina chose tuna on rye. Another man carried a cardboard box that held a mix of beverages. There was water, iced tea and several different sodas. Gina decided on iced tea.

After everyone had food, they found a spot to sit and eat. Many were sitting on the gravel parking lot. Gina hadn't wanted to, fearing she'd never be able to get back up again.

They sat around doing nothing and hearing nothing for another hour. Most people had their phones with them and were using them. Others stretched out and napped.

Gina watched another semi stop on the road out by the closed gate. Then it drove on. How many shipments had been lost today?

The people Gina sat near, weren't on their phones or napping. So, she decided to get information.

"How is the business doing, since Cory and Angie took over?" she asked.

"Hard to say," said Shawna. "The number of orders has increased. We're moving out more plants this year than last. Cory says business is booming. But there's no real way for me to tell, but it looks like it is."

"Things look good on the surface," said David. "They're

doing all the right things. I've only been here three years. Two years under Bob and one under Cory and Angie. And Dustin. They're putting money into repairs and maintenance. And the workers. Conditions have improved. Businesses with long-term health take care of their people. They're doing that. And branching out into new territory. Bob rarely did plants from bulbs. That's a big chunk of the early spring business. And Angie's almost cut out pesticide use. She's moved the business towards sustainability. Recycling water and fertilizer."

"You're wondering if Cory would blow up the business?" said Shawna

"I'm guessing Sheriff Jannson is," said Gina.

"I can see where he might think that," said Shawna. "But he's wrong. I've known Cory for years. I've worked with him in the greenhouses. He's not that kind of person. Even if he were in over his head, he'd come clean to everyone and ask for input. He's a teamwork sort of person."

"I hope you're right," said Gina. "But if he didn't do this, who did?"

"I have no idea," said Shawna, "but I'd love to get my hands on them. Threatening all our lives like this. It makes me so angry."

Gina saw fury in the woman's eyes.

"And our livelihoods," said David. "I'm trying hard not to think about all the plants that aren't getting watered. Or won't get shipped out on time."

"Yes," said Shawna. "So far, I've counted eight semis that have turned away because of the closed gate. And that's just today. And we've lost at least one greenhouse. All the glass has fallen and crushed plants. Who knows how many other greenhouses have fallen in?"

"It's going to be mess to clean up," said David. "I just want to get started. Sitting here is annoying."

"I know," said Shawna.

Sometime around four, Emily came over. She looked tired and her face and clothes were streaked with black, presumably from the smoke.

"In a few minutes, the deputies will begin taking some of us in to get our belongings. We don't know yet who will be allowed back in tomorrow. It depends on how long the investigation takes. Any time you've been scheduled, but can't get in the buildings to work, because of this, will be paid. Those who do come, like the field people, will be give time and a half, Cory says. But we don't know yet which greenhouses are stable enough to work in. All the propane tanks have blown from the fire, so there's no heat in any of the greenhouses. That might save some plants, since they won't dry out as fast. We have six people in the hospital. Trang, Juan, Eric, Jessica, John and Heather. Eric's the most serious. He has a badly broken leg. The others have broken arms, bad cuts and Heather and Juan both have head injuries. They've been admitted so the doctors can watch them, but it looks like they'll be okay. The other four have been released and gone home already. Not everyone is accounted for, we can't get to the computers to compare my list with who might have called in sick today. If you know of anyone, please talk to me so I can contact them and confirm they're not still in the building. The police have told us that they can't go into the buildings until the fire department okays it. The fire is finally out. That's about all I know," said Emily. Her face looked grim.

Three deputies came over and everyone walked down the

closed driveway on the right side of the complex, towards the back of the greenhouses.

The deputies divided them up into groups, depending on where their belongings had been left.

"Take Shawna and her group first," said David.

The others agreed.

Shawna and a group of six others followed a deputy inside. They were going to the center of the complex where they'd left jackets, keys and water bottles.

Gina had been alone. The others insisted she go next. Deputy Hammond took her to the greenhouse she'd been working in. Thankfully, the glass was still in place in most of the greenhouses they walked through. The plants unharmed.

Gina quickly packed up her supplies, dumped the paint water and got her chair. She went back outside with the Deputy, then walked alone to the parking lot.

What a mess. She loaded up her car and thought about going to look at the other side of the building. But she didn't really want to. The photos had been awful enough.

Shawna came out, carrying her coat and a water bottle.

"How did things look where you were?" Gina asked.

"Most of the greenhouses seem okay. At least three have lost all or part of their glass. The one next to the shipping area will need to be taken down and replaced. The supports are too twisted. I'm guessing any plants in a greenhouse that's lost glass are toast. Even if we went through each pot, picking out all that glass would take forever. We can't risk selling plants to customers that have glass in them."

Shawna shook her head, clearly near tears. Gina put her arms around the woman.

"I'm sorry. I know this is just hormones."

"No this isn't just hormones. This has been a horrible week. For all of us. The only reason I'm not crying is that I don't know people here that well. I'm not attached to them. And I haven't raised those plants from seeds or bulbs."

Shawna nodded.

"Are you all right to drive home?"

"I am. It's only five minutes."

"Okay. Take care of yourself tonight."

"I will. I think this would be a good day for a warm bath. With bubbles. And maybe I'll watch a fluffy movie afterwards."

"Perfect. I might do that myself," said Gina.

Both of them got into their cars and drove off.

When Gina got home, she texted Melanie that she was home and didn't need a ride.

Shall I pick up a pizza and come for dinner?

Gina rubbed her face. She didn't want pizza, but felt the need to talk.

Meet you at the Marina in half an hour?

Perfect. See you.

Gina set to work feeding the cats. She changed clothes and washed her face, just to freshen up. She ran her damp hands through her hair in an attempt to rearrange it and give it some life.

Then grabbed her small purse and checked to make sure she had everything: keys, wallet, phone. Gina was about to the car when she remembered. Coat. She slipped into her raincoat.

The Marina was ten minutes away. They'd be arriving at peak dinner hour on a Friday night. Oh well.

Melanie got there first. She'd been off work since four. The receptionist had seated her already.

Gina sat down and scanned the menu quickly. Misty came almost immediately to bring water and take their order.

"What'll you have tonight ladies?" she asked.

"I think tonight it's the Hoppy as a Clam ale and seafood pasta," said Melanie. "With the house dressing."

"I'll have the Barrel-aged Breakfast Stout and a fish burger," said Gina. "No fries."

"Do you want a salad or coleslaw instead?"

"Is the coleslaw fresh?"

"Always. Mitch makes it every morning."

"I'll have that then."

"Great. I'll be right back with your drinks." Misty left quickly, for once.

"I got the last empty table."

"Perfect timing," said Gina.

"You hungry?"

"Starving. I had a late lunch, a sandwich. But for some reason, I'm really hungry."

"So what happened today? I want to hear everything," said Melanie, leaning forward.

Gina was in the middle of telling Melanie about the day when Misty brought their beer.

"Oh, you're talking about the explosion. I heard rumors that Taylor Gardens is in debt and failing. And the person speculated that Cory is behind the murder and his sister's accident. Wants the insurance money all for himself."

Gina sipped her stout. The foamy rich and full-bodied beer slid down into her empty stomach. Blissful.

"Who told you that?" asked Melanie, looking casual.

"Someone who works there. I can't divulge my sources, but he's been there a long time. Long enough to know a lot of things."

"Aw c'mon," said Melanie. "You know I'm not going to tell anyone. I don't have a dog in this hunt."

"Okay, but don't tell anyone. He's worked there forever and I don't want him to lose his job. He's a trustworthy source of information."

Gina pretended disinterest and took another sip of her beer. She wanted Misty to keep talking, without prodding her.

"I don't know him," said Melanie.

The kitchen bell pinged.

"Well, I've gotta deliver an order." And Misty was off.

Melanie said, "Well?"

"I wouldn't believe him. But it's interesting that he's passing that around."

"Isn't it? Now back to your story."

Gina had just finished talking about her day when the food came.

She ate the coleslaw first, to get her daily veggies in. The fish burger was divine. Moist and tasty with lettuce, tomato and tartar sauce on a sesame seed bun. It was exactly what she needed.

"You *were* hungry," said Melanie, staring at Gina's empty plate. Melanie was only halfway through her meal.

"I was. What did they say on the news?"

"Just that it was a gas explosion. Well, at first they thought it was just a fire. The last report I heard on my way home from work was that there were at least six injuries and it wasn't known if anybody had been killed."

"So nothing beyond what we were told."

"How can they not know if anybody was killed?"

"The fire wasn't out. Many of the greenhouses were unstable. They might not be safe enough to go into."

"But you told me they keep records of who's on site."

"Visitors. The employees have a time clock."

"So couldn't they just check who clocked in that morning against who wasn't there at the end?"

"Emily was tracking who was there after the explosion. Electricity was out. I'm sure wiring was damaged. And I don't know what the state of the office is. Don't know if it got burned or if the computers were damaged. I assume the time clock was electric and hooked into the computers somehow. Maybe wireless, maybe not."

"So is someone trying to kill the three kids or just destroy Taylor Gardens?"

"That's the million-dollar question, isn't it?"

"And who would benefit from either of those choices? What's that saying on all the cop shows—follow the money."

"What if it's not about money?"

"There's a business involved. Doesn't that make it about money somehow?"

"It was at Ravenswood, wasn't it?" asked Gina.

"Yeah. There were other things involved, but basically the rare plants meant money," said Melanie.

"So, who would gain financially if Taylor Gardens went belly up?" asked Gina.

"Cory, right?"

"I assume so. I assume his dad would too. And Angie. All of the owners, don't know if there's more than that," said Gina.

"Bob's not married, right?"

"He's been divorced for decades. She might still be getting some money from him. No idea. Lives in California, I think."

"Okay, let's rule her out as highly unlikely."

Gina nodded.

"So that leaves the three of them. Anyone else?"

"I don't know who the owners are for sure."

"I heard Bob was tight with money. He's not a worker's coop sort of guy. I don't think he'd let an employee earn or buy a stake of the business. If he had, then he would have given them a management position before or when he retired," said Melanie.

"Okay, so back to the three of them. Well, Angie didn't blow anything up. So that leaves Cory or Bob. I just can't see either of them doing it."

"I can't either. But remember what Sheriff Jannson told us at Ravenswood. Not to believe in coincidences."

"Yeah, I agree. It's too far-fetched to think this is one."

Finally in the end, neither of them had a clue who had created the explosion. They planned to pay attention at the funeral and the reception the next day.

Gina finished her beer. It made her feel sleepy.

She went home, slipped her pajamas on, petted the cats and went to bed. She'd get up tomorrow and find out if the nursery was open.

SATURDAY MORNING

GINA WOKE LATE THE NEXT MORNING. SHE HAULED HERSELF OUT of bed and drank what felt like half the daily water requirement during the first thirty minutes. The beer from last night had dehydrated her.

There were no messages on her phone.

She fed the cats who'd been trying to wake her up for hours. They were miffed because she'd been gone so much this week. After their breakfast they both went to sit near the window to bathe. Pointedly ignoring her.

She made a cup of Irish Breakfast tea and looked out at the gray sky. It was 10 a.m. She should just give up on breakfast and go straight to lunch. There would be food at the reception.

Gina wasn't hungry, but she toasted an English muffin and spread cream cheese on both halves. Then turned on some folky music, hoping it would help her wake up, but gently.

After breakfast, she showered and dressed in black pants and a black blouse with a white floral design on it. The weather looked rainy out, so she wore her olive green raincoat, tucking the rain hat in a pocket. The funeral could be either outdoors or inside.

She filled a water bottle and got her purse. The cats were still ignoring her.

"I'll be back later, kids."

The cemetery was on the other side of the island, half an hour away. It was a nice drive on a beautiful spring day. Even if the sky was gray.

There were rhodies in bloom, some were the native purple variety, others a rainbow of colors planted in gardens she drove past. In the wildish areas, pink blooming currants dotted the landscape, along with the white flower of Indian plum shrubs. In a sunny spot, she saw a swath of pale-pink native bleeding heart, not as showy as the cultivated ones she'd been trying to paint yesterday These held a more delicate and subtle beauty.

Gina pulled up to the cemetery and parked at the end of the line of cars. There was a dark green canopy out among the graves, where people gathered.

Along the pathway, sat a white board upon which had been elegantly written *Dustin Taylor Services*. Gina joined the others standing beneath the canopy. Melanie wasn't there yet and although Gina recognized several people from around town, she didn't know anyone here yet, other than Bob and Cory.

The two of them were talking to the minister. Gina didn't know what church he was from. There were three on the island, but she wasn't a churchy person. She believed in the divinity of nature, but wasn't sure about God. She lumped herself in the agnostic category.

The cemetery grounds were formal. They contained

several stately deciduous trees, which were in the process of unfurling spring green leaves. Gina couldn't tell what kind they were. There were many older graves in the distance, with large upright headstones. Surrounding those were graves with newer headstones, rectangles set flush in the ground. Probably so mowers could go over them easily. A tall border of evergreen trees, mixed with twenty-foot tall ancient rhodies, formed the border on three edges. The fourth direction had a low hedge of what looked like clipped boxwood over which a view of Puget Sound could be seen.

Melanie arrived not much later. The crowd had swelled to forty or so people, many of them employees.

Gina saw Mckenzie, Emily and Carla arrive together. Jason came alone. He stood near Juan, Trang and Eric. David stood next to Shawna. She was holding hands with a pale-looking man wearing a dark jacket and conservative tie. Her partner, or husband, looked like he worked in an office.

Off to one side, stood Sheriff Jannson and Deputy Hammond. Why wasn't Sheriff Winters here? Now that was interesting. She certainly took a different approach to her work than Sheriff Jannson.

The ceremony wasn't long. The minister said what needed to be said and then was done. Gina doubted Dustin was a church-goer. She wasn't even sure that Bob or Cory were either.

Neither Bob or Cory spoke. They looked tired and strained. What a terrible week it had been for them both.

A woman who seemed to be Cory's wife stood behind them. She wore all black and looked thin and pale. A teenager, who looked like her mother, stood in front of her.

Afterwards, many people lined up to give their

condolences to the two men. Gina decided to wait until the reception.

She and Melanie stood talking and watching the crowd, but didn't discuss the past week.

Emily came up to them and said, "It's probably in bad taste to talk about work at a funeral, but if I tell you in person that's one less person I need to call tonight. The Fire Department's finishing up their investigation today. And Cory has called a staff meeting tomorrow at noon. He's going to talk about the future and is requiring all employees to be there. And no, I don't know what he's going to say. If it's not rainy, we'll meet in the courtyard. If it is, we'll meet in the first greenhouse, the one that's on the far right as you enter from the front. I don't know which door will be open, but I'll make it obvious tomorrow."

"I'll be there," said Gina.

"Thanks," said Emily. "That's only another hundred phone calls I need to make today."

"Make sure you get enough rest, please," said Gina.

"I hope to get some tonight. I'm really tired. I slept twelve hours last night. Well, I'm going to pay my respects and take off. I'm not going to the reception. Gotta get those calls done."

Mckenzie joined them a few minutes later.

"Are you going to the reception?" she asked.

"Yes, we are," said Gina. She introduced Melanie.

"Nice to meet you. Good. I'm glad you're going. I don't know anyone else here, but I really feel like I should go."

"Yes, you probably should. Part of being management," said Gina. "At least until Cory tells you otherwise."

"Do you think he'll close Taylor Gardens?"

"Your guess is better than mine," Gina said. "I really have no idea."

"Me neither. I sure hope he doesn't. I really want to just do my job. I like it there. Well, I did until all this happened."

Gina nodded in understanding.

As the crowd dwindled, Gina and Melanie walked to their cars. They lived at opposite ends of the island. The reception, at Bob's house, lay in the middle, so they said goodbye until they met there.

It took fifteen minutes to drive back to the center of the island. Rather it took five minutes to wait for everyone to turn around at the cemetery and ten minutes to drive to the reception.

Bob's house was a large old-fashioned two-story house. It was painted white with dark red trim and had a manicured, but otherwise very normal front yard. Grassy lawn punctuated with one tree on each side of the main sidewalk that ran from the house to the curb. Five-foot tall *Rhododendrons,* that were blooming in pink and red, hugged the house and partially blocked windows. In front of those sat several shorter evergreen shrubs. Gina saw no perennials at all. Just shrubs, trees and bark.

Bob was clearly a businessman, not a plantsman. And presumably, he hired out the maintenance.

Melanie drove up a minute later.

She looked at Gina, her mouth open in shock. Gina smiled.

"Oh my. I would have thought better of him. Hope he didn't entertain clients at home," said Melanie.

Melanie's taste ran to collector's plants. Especially to the wild and outlandish-looking ones.

They followed a few other people up the wooden steps to

the front door. The door opened and a woman wearing a black dress and pearls said, "Please come in."

The woman looked about Gina's and Melanie's age.

Gina followed the others inside. Melanie drifted off in search of the bathroom.

The inside of the house was painted completely white. The floors were hardwood. Most people had gathered in a large living room. The furniture looked mismatched, some pieces new and others a couple of decades old. There were no houseplants that Gina could see.

The paintings on the walls were all abstract and the colors were cool, leaving her feeling unsettled and unwelcome. They weren't comfortable art, but challenging. Not the sort of thing she would have had in her home. Perhaps Bob knew the artist.

"Horrid aren't they?" asked the older woman who'd been at the door.

"Well, they're not my taste."

"Mine either," the woman said. "I thought Bob bought them to spite me, but apparently, he liked them, since they're still up. I'm Sandra Wells, Bob's ex-wife and Dustin, Angie and Cory's mother." She held out her hand to shake.

Gina shook her hand.

"I'm so sorry for your loss."

"Thank you."

The woman had pronounced her name "Sondra." She looked elegant in a simple black dress and pearls, her chin-length sleek gray hair perfectly in place. Gina had noticed her at the funeral. She must have been one of the first to leave in order to get back here to open the house.

"I'm Gina Wetherby. I'm an artist. I recently got hired by

Taylor Gardens, although I believe I've known Bob for several years. Raven Island is a small place."

Sandra laughed. "Yes it is. One of the reasons why I left. Of course, it was much smaller forty years ago when I lived here."

"I haven't been here nearly that long," said Gina. "Where do you live now?"

"L.A. My husband is a producer. I've put some of my money into a few films as well. I like to support films about older women."

"Oh good. We need more of those. I get so tired of all the movies about kids. Life doesn't end at thirty."

"No, it certainly doesn't."

"Have you been back here much since you moved away?"

"Not once. The kids have always come down to see me. But I had to come for this. And to visit Angie in the hospital."

"How's she doing?"

"She's awake, thank goodness. They've just begun doing tests. She's disoriented, but they had her up walking this morning. She was doing fine, a little unsteady but she'll get there. She's a strong woman."

"I'm so relieved. I saw those hanging baskets fall on her. I was so afraid."

"You were there?"

"I was in the next greenhouse, painting, when the accident happened."

"And no one was messing with the line the baskets were hanging on."

"Not just before the accident."

"But before that?"

"Yes. A man was adjusting things. I told the police."

"Good. I sure hope they find who's doing this. The person who killed my Dustin and hurt Angie."

Sandra didn't look grief-stricken, rather in complete control. She looked fierce, like a mother bear protecting her cub.

"I do too. It's horrible."

"Have you worked there long?"

"I just started this week."

"I'll bet you think this was the wrong week to start," said Sandra.

"It's crossed my mind."

"Well, they'll catch the person. They have to."

"How long are you staying up here?"

"I'm not sure. I want to be there for Angie. She'll need help once she comes home. I'm a wretched cook, but I make a mean salad and I do know how to buy take out."

"She lives alone then? I just met her the morning of the accident."

"Yes, she lives for her work. There's no room for a partner when you're as driven as she is, at least for right now."

Bob and Cory had come in the front door and were deluged by people.

"Well, I'd better get to the kitchen and check on the food situation. It was lovely meeting you. Maybe we can get together for coffee sometime. I don't know anyone here, except the family. And their conversation is only about work."

"I'd love too," said Gina. She gave Sandra one of her cards.

"Wonderful cards. This is your art, I assume."

"Yes."

"It's beautiful. I can see why Bob and Cory wanted to hire you."

Sandra tucked her card into a dress pocket and wove through the crowd towards the kitchen.

When had they begun making dresses with pockets again? What a terrific thing.

Gina moved into the dining room. There was a side table set up with coffee and hot water. Gina found some mint tea in a group of miscellaneous packets. She opened it, took out the bag and poured hot water over it.

"A teetotaler I see," said Jason, coming up beside her and pouring a cup of coffee.

She laughed quietly and said, "I do have the occasional drink, but coffee doesn't agree with me anymore. Tea always does."

He shook his head, "Awful business, this."

She really disliked Jason, but he was being polite and trying to make small talk, so she would too. What had her mother always said? "You catch more flies with honey than vinegar."

"Yes, it is. Do you think Cory will reopen?"

"I don't know. I wouldn't. I'd throw in the towel and retire early. Spend time with my family. But he's younger than I am. Still, money isn't everything."

"No, it isn't. Do you have family?"

"No. I never dated. Was always too busy working or recovering from work."

"But your work is highly seasonal. Wouldn't you have time to date in the fall or winter?"

"Time yes, but I never found the right woman."

"Well, there is that. If Cory closes, what will you do?"

"I don't know. Probably try to get a job elsewhere."

"Will that be difficult, this late in the season?"

"I don't know that, either. It's been a very long time since I looked for work. But I've got a lot of experience. It should count for something. What will you do?"

"I'm retired and not dependent on the money. Painting is my second career, so I'll just keep painting and sell the paintings."

They had moved away from the beverages, so other people could get to them. Sheriff Jannson had come in and poured a cup of coffee.

He turned to join them and said, "Oh, this is what I needed."

"Good coffee, isn't it?" asked Jason.

The doors to the kitchen opened and two young women came out, each carrying a platter of food. They set them on the white tablecloth, then returned to the kitchen and brought out more.

After six more trips, the table was completely full of food. Gina stood in line, taking a clean white plate from the stack with her empty hand. She set it down on the empty edge of the table and took a couple of the finger sandwiches, some carrot sticks and bell pepper strips. Then spooned some of the veggie dip onto her plate. And added a couple of crackers with cream cheese and smoked salmon on top. There was a sideboard full of desserts. She'd come back later for those. Maybe.

She retreated to the living room and took a seat on the modern-looking sofa, only because there was a coffee table in front of it. The sofa was as uncomfortable as it looked.

"May I?" Sheriff Jannson asked, looking at the empty space next to her.

"Certainly," she said.

He sat down and began eating. His plate was nearly overflowing.

After a few minutes, he said, "I skipped breakfast."

"Why?"

"No time this morning."

"Did something happen?"

"No, Sheriff Winters wanted to confer."

"How is she doing?"

"Frustrated that people won't talk to her."

"I'm not surprised."

"Do you think it's racism?" he asked.

"Maybe with a few people, but not most. More likely, it's her manner."

"I told her that, but she's bristly. She won't listen to me."

"That's a pity."

"Maybe you could talk to her."

"Me? I don't think she'll listen to me. I'm a suspect, right?"

"No. She's crossed you off her list."

"Well good. I can't even seem to kill slugs. I'm reduced to tossing them over the fence to the neighbors who don't garden."

"That's a terrible thing," he said, arching his eyebrow at her.

She'd decided that was his signal he was joking.

"They don't care. They're putting their energy into remodeling the house. They'll even be taking all their lawn out this summer and putting in a patio pavers. Sound thinking if you ask me. I've never liked lawns."

"Waste of good planting space?" he asked.

"Well yes, but more it's a waste of water and in most cases people who don't garden use weed and feed and other horrible chemicals on their lawns. Polluting the environment and killing far too many beneficial insects. Monoculture at its worst."

"There you go, throwing those big words at me." He grinned at her.

"I guess I feel rather strongly about it."

"I like that. There are worse things to feel strongly about."

"So how's the investigation going?"

"Chugging along," he said, evasively.

"But no breaks?"

He smiled at her.

"Let's not talk about work, okay?" he said.

"What do you want to talk about?" she asked.

"This fine, fine potato salad."

"I didn't have any. But the egg salad sandwiches are divine. It's curried."

"Mmm." he said, taking another bite of potato salad and closing his eyes.

Mckenzie sat on the other side of her. She had no plate and wasn't drinking anything.

"I didn't realize there would be food," she said. "I stopped for a burger on the way here. I've never been to a funeral before."

"It's common if there's a reception at one's house," said Gina. "It used to be that people's church members and friends would show up with food and sometimes drinks, to celebrate the deceased's life."

"Sort of like a wake?" asked Mckenzie.

"Yes, but usually without the alcohol. I don't think it's as common anymore. Us Americans aren't very comfortable with death."

"And other places are?" she asked.

"I think they are."

"I've gotta travel more, both of us do," said Mckenzie. "Steph just looked at me like I had two heads when I asked if she wanted to come today."

"Understandable."

"I know, right? I kept asking myself why I was coming."

"To show respect and support for the living," said Gina.

"That's all I could come up with, too. I wasn't fond of Duncan," she whispered.

"I had just met him. But I have known Bob for a while. And I quite like Cory and Angie," said Gina.

Mckenzie said, "Oh, there's Cory. I think I'll go pay my respects and leave. Is it too soon?"

"I think it's fine."

Mckenzie was just looking for permission from someone.

Jason and Bob came into the room and sat on the other side of the coffee table. Bob looked exhausted, but was putting on a good front. They were talking about fishing and seemed very chummy.

Jason was a conundrum. Ever since she'd met him, he'd been polite and charming. Except on the first day. When he'd made no secret of his dislike for Dustin. Other people had said it was sour grapes, him being passed over as Bob's kids got the management positions. Yet she'd never heard him refer to that, but she didn't know him that well. He was clearly good at hiding his true feelings.

"Penny for your thoughts," said Sheriff Jannson.

Funny how she thought of him as Sheriff Jannson, rather than Bryan, whenever he was in uniform.

"Just musing on people's abilities to hide what's going on inside."

"Bob or Jason?" he asked.

"Both, I think."

"You are good."

She looked at his plate. It was empty.

"You were hungry."

"Told you. I didn't have time for breakfast and this is lunch. Who knows about dinner? It might not happen either. Nothing is certain when I'm on duty."

"If Sheriff Winters works out, when will you retire?"

"Maybe two months. We'll make a mutual decision. I don't think it will be long. She'll want me out of her hair."

"Are you ready for that?"

"I don't know. I've never been retired before. I'll need to find some things to do this time, but I'm looking forward to that. After I spend a week or two of doing nothing."

"I can't picture you doing nothing."

"I'm surprisingly good at it," he said. "I'm going to get some dessert. Before someone tracks me down and finds something I need to deal with."

He got up.

Gina finished eating her vegetables. The dig was tangy and filled with cilantro. She loved it.

Melanie sat down in the empty spot next to her.

"Not eating?" asked Gina.

"No. I'm saving up. Going out to eat tonight."

"Where?"

"Fancy place over on the mainland. Called Bijou."

"Ooh, who with?"

"A guy from Seattle. Landscaper. He came by the nursery

last week. Again. We've been friends online for years. In a geeky plant group."

"Interesting. And you feel safe?"

"Wouldn't go if I didn't. You know that."

"I know. It's just meeting someone online."

"No, we met in person. At a plant lecture. Then became friends. And we're both in the same online group and kept stumbling over each other. Plus he's come out to Ravenswood several times a year for years now. And he has good taste in plants."

"He must have a spectacular garden," said Gina.

"He rents a basement from some friends. He has a teensy vegetable garden in their yard. The plants he buys are for clients."

"You're kidding?"

Melanie shook her head.

"Wow. I would think a landscaper would have their own garden."

"He's been saving up for decades to buy a large chunk of property, in cash. In Seattle. Hard to find and hard to afford anything there."

"Well that's true. I don't know anyone who can afford Seattle these days. What does it take now, an income of about $100,000 a year?"

"More," said Melanie. "for a medium-priced house. Which doesn't include much land."

"I'm so glad we bought out here, when we did."

"Me too."

"But if we hadn't, I'd still have a house in Seattle. On Capital Hill, where prices are through the roof. I'd be so rich."

Melanie laughed.

"So when he does buy the property, when will he have time to garden? I know what sort of hours many landscapers work."

"He's retiring in August."

"Interesting. So, he must be planning on finding that patch of land soon."

"Yep. Well, we'll see what happens."

"You've never mentioned him before. You've mentioned the Facebook group, but not him."

"Never thought he'd ask me out on a date."

"When?"

"He came by the nursery yesterday."

"And you didn't mention it last night?"

"We were distracted by events at hand."

"Sorry," said Gina. "I sort of monopolized things."

"No apology needed. And I don't know if this will work or not, so I didn't really want to talk about it. Well, I think I'm going to take my anxious self home and go try to get the dirt out from under my fingernails or something."

"Deep breaths. And no man's worth it if he doesn't love the dirt under your fingernails."

Melanie laughed. She got up and left.

Gina decided she'd get some dessert and try to talk to Bob and Cory.

She found Cory hanging out at the dessert table.

"How are you doing?" she asked.

"I'm okay. Making a decision helped a lot. And no, I won't tell you what it is until the meeting tomorrow. It takes a long explanation."

She nodded.

"I heard Angie's doing better."

His face lit up.

"I'm so relieved. I think she's gonna be okay. They're not a hundred percent sure yet, but I've gotta think positively about this."

"Good. Do the police have any clue who's behind all this?"

"If they do they haven't told me. Sheriff Winters must be a mean poker player."

"That's what I thought."

"I'm still not sure she's ruled me out as a suspect. I wouldn't hurt Angie for anything. Or the business. And I certainly wouldn't have my little brother murdered."

Cory seemed disturbed that someone would think him capable of those things.

"Well, she doesn't know you. And she's a stranger here. Until they catch someone, I think they consider everyone a suspect."

Cory nodded, his mouth full of a lemon bar.

Gina looked at the desserts. Surprisingly, nothing looked good. The chocolate cake at her house sounded better. So did solitude.

"I'm really sorry about Dustin," she said.

"Thanks. I'm going to miss him. Even though he enjoyed being a thorn in my side. He kept me honest and humble."

Someone else came up to talk to him, so Gina went off in search of Bob. He was in the hallway, talking to Sandra.

"I'm so sorry, both of you, about Dustin."

"Thank you. He was a wonderful son. And I'll call you for coffee," she said, patting her pocket with Gina's business card in it.

"Good."

"I'm sorry you got dragged into all this, Gina. It's a real mess," said Bob.

"Well, at least Angie's awake."

"Yes, I'm glad. And Cory's safe. I hope they catch the bastard soon. Pardon my English."

"No pardon needed. I hope so too."

Someone else was leaving and was waiting to speak to Bob. Gina went out the front door. The breeze felt almost warm. The sun was out. It was a lovely spring afternoon.

She drove home. Then walked around the garden to see what was happening. Her *Dicentra 'Goldheart'* was up a few inches. The new growth looked like gnarled pinkish-red fingers coming up through the soil. She loved the plant in all its stages.

In another bed, her *Epimedium 'Pink Champagne'* was blooming. The plant, also called fairy wings, held its delicate pink and raspberry-colored flowers high, letting them dangle in the breeze. She loved it and had decided to tuck more varieties of *Epimedium* in the shady spots in her garden.

The sun went behind a neighbor's tall cedar tree and the temperature felt like it dropped ten degrees.

She hadn't had the energy or time to watch a fluffy movie last night. But tonight, she would. Gina didn't want to think about the meeting tomorrow. Or the murder, accident and explosion.

Tonight, she was going to have a piece of chocolate cake, then a glass of wine and watch movies with the cats.

THE COURTYARD WAS FULL OF EMPLOYEES. GINA HAD NEVER SEEN some of them before. It was a bright sunny morning, full of promise.

But no one looked like it was. Nearly everyone was waiting, speaking in hushed voices and expecting Cory to announce they were closing.

Gina arrived early, eager to find out Cory's decision. She'd sat at one of the few tables and was glancing through the piled-up email on her phone. Shawna sat next to her and Mckenzie across the table.

Shawna asked, "What time is it?"

"Noon," said Gina.

"He's late. Cory's never late," said Mckenzie. "How can he be late at a time like this?"

At 12:05 p.m. Cory walked out from behind the first greenhouse, obviously having just come from his car. Everyone stopped talking.

"Sorry I'm late. I was on an important phone call. Trying to get some last minute details so I could share them with all of you."

He set his laptop and water bottle down on a table and shrugged his jacket off.

"Okay, first I wanted to update you on Angie. She's up and walking. Better today than yesterday. The doctors are confident she'll be steady on her feet in a couple of days. Her speech comes in chunks. She sometimes forgets what you've just told her, but that's getting better too. There's a really good chance she'll recover completely. And sooner than the docs originally thought."

Everyone clapped. It seemed Angie was well-liked by everyone or if she wasn't, no one was willing to admit it. Even Jason clapped.

Cory continued.

"So that's the good news. The bad news is that we've got no heat in any of the greenhouses. If it continues to stay warm, the plants should be fine, just a little behind. If we get a late cold snap, they won't. I've closed greenhouse doors and vents to hold the heat in.

"The shipping area is a total loss. Miraculously, there were no fatalities. Six people were injured. Only one is still in the hospital, Eric. He should be released sometime next week, but a broken leg is temporarily disabling, even for someone young.

"Two other greenhouses, the ones closest to the shipping greenhouse, will need to be taken down. Insurance may or may not pay for replacements. The insurance company is doing their own investigation. One greenhouse has lost all its glass, the other still has some of the glass falling. The plants in both of those greenhouses will need to be trashed. We won't compost anything. The risk of someone getting cut, even with tempered glass, is just too high."

Gina listened. It didn't sound like Cory was planning on closing.

"The gas-lines are destroyed. The fire department has determined they were tampered with. The police are still continuing to investigate. And while they are, a decision has to be made. The office, break room and restrooms are also a total loss. We didn't lose any computer data as everything is always backed up to the cloud."

Cory ran his hand through his unruly hair.

"You are the heart and soul of this company. Dad started it and built it up. Dustin, Angie and I have tried to continue his work and expand on it with our own skills. Angie and I talked about things this morning and came to a decision. We really want to keep going. But with a different model.

"We'd like to make this company worker owned. We haven't worked everything out yet. And it probably won't go into full effect until January. But we've got plans. First off, it would require us making sure we could employ people year round. We'd need fall and winter crops. The obvious choice for winter would be living Christmas trees. Of varying sizes and varieties. We'd need to start growing conifers and soon. We haven't figured out the fall season completely.

"We've also decided that we won't have gas or propane to heat the greenhouses anymore. It's just too unsafe. For years Angie has badgered Bob, and then me, to make the shift to solar panels or to investigate wind turbines. I think this is the time to make that investment. I don't know how much insurance will cover. Also we've completely lost four days of shipping plants. By the time we're up to speed again, those orders may be cancelled. Plus two entire greenhouses of plants will need to be trashed. All of you will be paid for time lost. Your paychecks will arrive as usual.

"So, we're up against a huge time crunch with substandard facilities until things can be rebuilt. And possibly bad weather. Angie and I want to move forward. But we'll really need your help.

"Without you, Taylor Gardens is just a dream. We need all of you to be flexible and show up on time as usual. To work hard and be willing to put in overtime. You'll be well paid for it. In the next month we'll be putting together a board of interested people to help us draw up plans for making this a worker owned business. Angie and I have always believed that life should be about more than just piling up more money, once you've got enough to live comfortably. We want to create something that benefits everyone. And we need your input.

"Tomorrow morning, we'll be open. We're having a trailer brought in today that will be the temporary office. Go there, first thing, and sign in. The old time clock's gone. We won't have a refrigerator for lunches, or an official break room for a week or so. They could only get us one trailer immediately, more are coming. We'll take care of getting the break room up and running as soon as we possibly can. This afternoon, I'll be getting a space together for shipping. Any of you who want a couple of hours overtime are welcome to stay and help me move things around.

"Now, I understand many of you are feeling a bit anxious about returning to work. I can't blame you. I can't imagine what that explosion was like. If you'd like to quit, just tell Emily on your way out. I won't force anyone to continue working here and I won't make you give two weeks' notice. That would be cruel.

"I don't want to pressure anyone, but if I could see a quick show of hands from those interested in moving forward with us."

Gina didn't raise her hand, she wasn't really an employee here. Just a contractor.

She looked around and couldn't see anyone who wasn't raising their hand. Cory looked relieved.

"Thank you for your faith in us. Angie will be so excited. It's all the docs can do to keep her in the hospital. Like I said, stick around if you want and we'll get that new shipping area set up so we can load up those incoming trucks tomorrow morning. Get those plants on their way."

Cory rubbed his face.

"Oh. Does anyone have questions? I can't answer anything about the worker-owned stuff until we make a board and meet and talk about what people want to do. But I can talk about other things.

"Are we going to ship out unwatered plants tomorrow?" asked Shawna.

"No. The water lines are working and I'll be watering this afternoon and tonight by flashlight if I have to. I know which plants are going out first. Unfortunately, we'll be shipping newly-watered plants if I'm doing it tonight, which we try not to do. The truckers don't like it, but we've no choice. We'll get as far ahead of that as we can tomorrow morning."

Someone else asked, "Are the police even close to catching the person who tried to blow us up? Is it safe to be here?"

"I don't know where the police are in their investigation. I don't believe they've arrested anyone. I can tell you there's no gas left to explode. The propane tanks have been hauled away and disposed of. The shipping area and the unstable greenhouses have been clearly roped off. No one is allowed inside them. After the insurance investigator arrives tomorrow, they will be torn down. I don't know when work will begin on new structures. I've only had a day and a half to get as far as I have with planning. We'll rebuild the shipping area first, then the greenhouses. Since we're moving into late spring, we'll need greenhouses less, until next winter. I want to be clear, I can guarantee no one's safety. Although the police believe that Angie and I, our family, are the targets. Not any of you. I feel terrible that anyone has been injured, or threatened. If you have any information, please share it with the police. We need to catch who's responsible."

"What should we do if we want to be on the board?"

Cory looked thoughtful for a moment and said, "Emily, can you start a list of people?"

She nodded.

"Give your name to Emily. We won't be meeting for a month or so. I want to focus on getting shipping back on track and things repaired first. After we have a temporary office, I'll put a clipboard out that people can put their name down on. Next to the sign-in sheet."

No one else asked a question.

"Well, if there's no more questions, then thank you all for coming. I'll see you tomorrow if you're scheduled. I'm so grateful for all of your help and energy for moving forward. It's going to be hard work, but I think we're going to make it."

People clapped and many seemed reluctant to leave. They gathered in clumps and began talking.

A couple of people went up to Cory, speaking to him

privately. Shawna got up and began to leave. Then she turned back to Mckenzie and Gina.

"This sort of puts a damper on my plans to have an off season to have the baby in. But I'm relieved they're planning on going year round. Don't know how I'll swing it, though," Shawna said.

"How are you with computers?" asked Mckenzie.

"Pretty good."

"We'll have a lot of planning to do. Lots of computer work to add in those extra seasons. I wonder if we'll need another office person."

Shawna brightened.

"Maybe you can even bring the baby. Until she's too old and needs to be entertained. Or maybe you could work from home. Talk to Cory," said Mckenzie.

"I will," she said. "But I'll do it another day. When he's not so rushed to get the shipping set up and water those plants."

Shawna left to go to her car.

Mckenzie said, "I had no idea this was the way they were going to go. I'm stunned, but excited. Using solar and wind power to grow our plants—that's a huge selling point." She grinned.

"I think it's wonderful. A couple of my friends have put solar panels on their houses. Now they're earning money that goes to lowering their electric bills. One of them is even selling excess electricity back to the power company," said Gina.

"Wonderful. I'm so excited about all this. I just hope we can get things repaired by the open house in June."

"A little over two months? Who knows?" asked Gina

Cory came over to them.

"I don't know what to work on first," said Mckenzie.

"Maybe some press releases to the trade websites. And local newspapers. Let them know we're not dead and have plans for the future. You have a computer?"

"I've always just used my laptop. I like it better than the old ones in the office."

"Well, we'll have new ones, but until then, press releases and keep working on the open house."

"Will we be rebuilt by then?"

"I don't know. But we'll sure try."

"Okay. I might spend tomorrow morning at home working. Then come here in the afternoon to check in. Since they'll be setting up the office."

"Good idea. Carla's going to buy office furniture tomorrow morning and try to get it delivered tomorrow. Then I'll have to pull a couple of people from somewhere to get it all put together. I'm sure it won't be pre-made."

"Great. Well, I'm off home to work on press releases. I'll email them so you can approve them."

"Wonderful, thanks Mckenzie."

Mckenzie got up and left. Cory sat down in her chair.

"I noticed you didn't raise your hand. Are you having second thoughts about working for us?"

"I'm not a regular employee, so I didn't think the vote applied to me," said Gina. "I'm happy to keep painting plant tags."

"What if we did want to hire you as a permanent employee?"

"I don't think you have that much work for me, do you?"

"I don't know. If we're going to add in two more seasons, we'll need more plant tags. And if we add in a fall season, we'll need to do a whole educational aspect. We'll need people to give talks to community groups, libraries and that sort of thing about planting in the fall and how much better it is around here. Those teaching will need art for brochures and PowerPoint presentations. I have other plans, but we can talk about those some other time. I think we'll be able to use you a lot."

"I'll need to think about that. I do value my retirement."

"Maybe you won't have to work full time once you've caught up, maybe only a few hours a week. Let's talk about it again after you've done the plant tags we agreed upon. I just wanted to make sure you knew that if you want, you can be one of the owners of this company too."

"Thank you. I'll give it some thought. I'm pleased to hear about Angie."

"Me too. It's such a relief she'll be okay."

"What does your dad think about these changes?"

"He thinks we're crazy, but said he'll go along with them. He never wanted to use anything except propane. But he's old school and admits it. Thinks it's an expense that won't pay off. Angie's done the calculations that it will. She has data, he doesn't. I think it's time to get ahead of the curve. And really, could I ask anyone here to walk back into work if we replaced the gas lines and got new propane tanks? Everything was as protected as we could make it without posting a twenty-four hour guard. I never want to put people at risk like that again."

Gina nodded.

"I think it's a good choice."

"Well, I better get into the greenhouses and start setting up the shipping area. While I've still got help," Cory said, getting up. "See you tomorrow?"

"Yes. I've got photos to take and paintings to paint."

"Good," he said, leaving to gather up the group of people who were waiting for him.

Gina walked to her car.

She'd be back tomorrow, but hoped the police were making progress on their investigation. Someone seemed determined to either kill the Taylor family or the business. She still wasn't sure which.

MONDAY MORNING

GINA FOUND HERSELF BACK IN THE SAME GREENHOUSE AS FRIDAY. Still trying to paint the bleeding hearts before they left for stores.

Yesterday, the sun had warmed things up and Cory had all the greenhouse vents closed. The fans were running, keeping air moving in some of the greenhouses. Electrical work was still being done on some of them. It was going to take a while to replace all the damaged wiring.

Gina didn't understand how everything worked, she just knew this greenhouse was warmer than last Friday. Some of the others were cooler and the annuals were suffering. As soon as this one was emptied, which would be this afternoon, any sulking annuals would be put in here.

She'd already opened the watercolor block to a clean sheet and done a new wash. It had dried some and Gina began adding in more and more detail.

The plants had been watered this morning. The *Dicentra*

she chose to paint, still had water droplets on the leaves and drooping red and white blossoms.

People were coming and going. The place seemed busier and more energetic than last week. There was a lot of rearranging of plants and shipping going on. Many people had added extra work days to their schedule, eager for overtime. Extra delivery trucks had been planned.

She felt a sense of controlled chaos surrounding her. Cory had given her an updated shipping schedule marked with the greenhouse letters that the plants were in.

Gina had decided to paint these two bleeding hearts and then go hunt down plants for photos. The next ones she didn't have photos of shipped out tomorrow.

She finished the first painting and lay it aside on the concrete to dry. Then put that plant back in place. She looked at the yellow-leaved *Dicentra*, turning it, trying to decide which side to paint. One side looked fuller, another dramatic. This variety was all about drama, so she chose that side.

There was whooping and hollering coming from the direction of the courtyard. A crowd had gathered. Gina walked to the end of the greenhouse to get closer.

She saw Angie surrounded by people. The tall woman looked a bit paler than normal, but she was walking along just fine, barely using the cane she held.

Gina smiled, happy to see her back. She probably wouldn't be working in the greenhouse as usual, not with a cane. But it was clear Angie buoyed everyone's spirits. Well, possibly not everyone. Whoever had caused the accident probably wasn't happy to see her.

Gina walked back to her painting. She needed to get going. She was behind her normal goal. Year ago, when she'd first begun to paint Gina decided to do two paintings a day on most days in order to learn faster. And she was way behind what was needed if she wanted to stay on top of this job. Or even just a little behind. There were more plants scheduled to go out than she could paint in a day. It was time to up her game.

It took about an hour to do the second painting. By then her stomach was rumbling.

Gina pulled out her lunch and sat in the chair she'd brought. She'd made a turkey wrap out of lunchmeat, cream cheese and some spicy mustard greens she was growing in her back yard.

The mustards were purple with a bit of green showing through. A beautiful plant as well as tasty. She'd planted them last fall and they overwintered, so she'd picked some of the new smallish leaves. The bigger the leaves got, the larger their pepperiness. These small ones still had a bite.

She sipped iced tea from her second water bottle. Mint tea mixed with black. The mint cooled her mouth a bit from the greens. The black tea would keep her awake.

After lunch, she packed up the dry paintings, collapsed her easel and packed everything up, setting the supply bag on her chair.

Then she set out with the shipping list and her cell phone to take photos. She took photos out of order, beginning with the plants she found first. It took hours to search out all the plants. Her feet ached, even though she was wearing her most comfortable shoes. Running shoes were always the best.

Finally, she'd found them all. It was after four and she'd been here since eight in the morning.

Shipping was working later today than usual. So were the people who were shifting plants between greenhouses.

Everyone was working extra hard and extra hours to get plants out and keep the ones still on site looking their best.

The day had been uneventful, other than Angie's arrival. Gina had gotten two paintings done and a dozen more plants photographed. A good day's work.

She stepped outside near the new shipping greenhouse, the farthest one down on the burnt out side of the building. The two in front on that side would be torn down.

Outside this one, rows of rolling shelves laden with plants stood, waiting for a semi to arrive that would take them to whatever store the order was supposed to go.

Down near the burned-out old shipping area, Cory stood talking to a man in a suit. The insurance investigator? Possibly.

She hoped the company would wrap this up quickly and cut him a check. With all his plans, they'd need cash quickly. Putting up new greenhouses and all those solar panels wouldn't come cheap. Plus he was paying out a lot of overtime in order to get caught up.

Well, it was time for her to go home. Her feet hurt even though she sat all morning while painting. She'd give them a good rest tonight.

Tomorrow she'd need to photograph just as much. And Wednesday. Thursday and Friday, the shipping schedule was back to normal. If all went well. Gina hoped it would.

She returned to the greenhouse where her stuff was. Hefted the art bag up to her shoulder and collapsed the chair. She walked out past the courtyard, into a front greenhouse and out through that one to the parking lot.

Gina put all her things into the car and then went to the new trailer they'd brought in today and parked next to the old fire-damaged office.

Mckenzie sat at a desk, glowering at a computer screen when Gina walked in. In another corner, one of the workers was attaching a wheeled base to a chair. Angie was working at a keyboard.

Mckenzie looked up.

"Gina, how was your day?"

"Good. I got two paintings done and I've got everything photographed that went out today and that's leaving tomorrow morning."

"Go you. I'm waiting for technology to do its thing."

"Is that one still not updated?" asked Angie.

"I think you're hogging the internet," said Mckenzie.

Angie laughed.

"I am, aren't I? One more place to get a quote from and then I'm done for the day," said Angie, laughing.

"This place is a hive of industry today," said Gina.

"The office or everywhere here?" asked Mckenzie.

"Everywhere," said Gina.

"Good. Cause we've got to get caught up. Spring is busy enough, but being behind just adds to the pressure," Mckenzie said.

"Well, I just came to sign out. I'm going home to go rest my feet."

"Good. Go take care of yourself," said Mckenzie. "When do we get to see the paintings?"

"I was going to ask Cory what he wants me to do with them. I've only got a few so far, but they'll begin stacking up soon," Gina said.

Angie said, "I think we should scan them, for the tags first. Then get them framed and hang them up in our new office. I know Cory wants to build a larger one and add in a retail area.

We do get groups, mostly gardeners, who want to tour the greenhouses. Cory wanted to sell t-shirts, mugs, that sort of thing. With our logo."

"Some of the paintings might work well as t-shirts or mugs. Or you could have prints done and sell them. Even sell the originals if they were framed nicely," said Gina.

Angie leaned back in her chair, her mouth hanging open.

"None of that had occurred to either of us. But you're right. The garden groups would probably love that. Would you be all right with that?" asked Angie.

"Well, you own the paintings. You paid for them," said Gina.

"I've seen it as buying the rights to use the paintings. And you owning the paintings," said Angie. "We don't have a contract for you, do we?"

"No, just an agreement. I told Cory I wanted to do some paintings and see how all of you liked them first."

Angie said, "Well, how about we look at what you've got Friday morning and come to an agreement. Cory should have some time to breathe by then."

"Perfect," said Gina. "Once the shipping schedule gets more normal, I'll have less plants to photograph and more time to paint. Although I'm going to fall behind on the weekends. I can't work seven days a week like some of you."

"I can't either," said Angie. "No one can really. Even Cory falls apart after a few weeks. Last year I forced him to take some days off. You go put your feet up and I'll finish up getting solar panel bids so Mckenzie can get her new computer updated. Why they don't sell them already up to date is beyond me. Sheesh."

Gina laughed.

She went to her car and drove home. The weather felt almost balmy. It was probably close to sixty. She was looking forward to summer weather again and recovering from a winter of cold rain and dark days.

At home, Gina washed her brushes and lay today's paintings out with the others. Not much to show for a week's worth of work. Most of it spent not working. Maybe she'd do another one tonight.

She slipped her shoes and socks off and walked around barefoot. Her aching feet felt relieved.

She put in a load of laundry and looked in the fridge to consider dinner options. Then the freezer.

The cats circled around her legs, stepping on her bare feet and meowing.

"I know. You first."

She opened a can of cat food and divided it between the two bowls, setting them on the floor. Then she opened the fridge and perused its meager and uninteresting contents.

Her phone buzzed, still in the vest pocket.

"Hello,"

"Hi, what are you doing for dinner?" asked Sheriff Jannson.

"Looking at the boring food in my fridge," she said.

"I'm just outside Corvid. Should I pick up a pizza and come over? I don't know if you even like pizza."

"Oh, that sounds terrific. I love their pizza."

"What do you want on it?" he asked.

"How about their garlic lover's pizza? With Canadian bacon added to it. I've got some red wine we could open. If you're not on shift."

"Just got off. I'll limit myself to one glass, just in case. I'll be there as soon as the pizza's ready."

"Great," she said and hung up, plugging her phone in. The battery was low after all those photos.

Gina went into the bathroom and splashed some water on her face and tried, unsuccessfully, to do something with her hair. She'd dropped some of her lunch on the shirt. So she changed into a clean t-shirt and smoothed her hair down again.

Then went into the main room and tidied up some of the piles of mail and other papers that always seemed to accumulate. She cleaned off the kitchen table and put out two plates, silverware and napkins. Got out two wine glasses and opened the wine so it could breathe.

She should make a salad. That would be healthy.

From the fridge Gina pulled out lettuce, carrots, a bell pepper and three salad dressings. She slipped on her garden clogs and went out the sliding glass door to pick a few mustard greens. They needed to be eaten before the plants bolted.

Back inside, she rinsed everything and tore the greens into bite-sized pieces. She chopped the peppers and grated the carrots. Then tossed everything and put it into a serving bowl. She put the bowl and dressings on the table. Along with the wine.

Gina glanced at the time. It had been forty-five minutes. He should be here by now. Or have called to cancel.

The cats were sitting on the couch staring at her. Wondering what was up.

Gina poured herself a glass of wine and sat on the couch with her feet up. The wine was complex, fruity and strong. Just what she needed.

There was a knock at the door. She hauled herself up off the couch and put her glass on the table.

Gina opened the door and saw Bryan carrying two huge pizza boxes. He wasn't alone. There were also Sheriff Winters and a teenage boy, who looked embarrassed to be there. Probably her son.

"I brought company. Hope you don't mind, but they were waiting to get in to Corvid's and it was jammed," said Bryan. "They were never going to get in to eat before closing."

"Wonderful," said Gina. "You're all welcome here. Come on in."

They came in and she shut the door.

"I'll get some more plates," said Gina.

"This is Elijah, my son. Elijah, this is Mrs. Wetherby."

"Nice to meet you ma'am," he said, holding out his hand.

She shook it and said, "Gina. You can call me Gina.

Then saw his eyes get huge.

"Are those cats alive?" he asked.

"Yes."

"They're so big."

"They're Maine Coon cats. They get big."

"Can I pet them?" he asked.

"Absolutely, let me introduce you. The black one with gray tips is Albert. The orange and white cat is Alice. They love to be petted."

He tentatively reached out and petted Albert's head. Albert stood and leaned into the boy's hand.

"He likes it," said Elijah, grinning.

"Yes, he does.

"Elijah's aunt has three cats, but they're skittish around strangers. Still, I think he's won them over. But she lives in Chicago, so he's in need of a cat fix," said Sheriff Winters, smiling. "I told him we can get a cat once we're settled.

It was the first time Gina had seen her smile.

"It must be hard being so far away from family."

"Yes, but I think the schools are better out here."

"The animal shelter here always has a lot of cats and kittens that need homes."

"We'll look there when it's time. Thank you for the kind tip," said Sheriff Winters. "Although I am trying to talk my sister into moving out here and in with us. Then we'll have her cats."

Gina saw that Bryan had gotten out extra plates and silverware. In front of one place setting was a plastic bottle of soda. He'd opened both pizza boxes on the counter.

"I think we're ready to eat."

"I'm starving," said Gina.

They all got pizza and sat down. Gina dished up some salad and used blue cheese dressing on hers.

"Take some salad," Sheriff Winters said to her son.

"Should I call you Sheriff Winters?" asked Gina.

"No. My name's Ivy."

"I'm glad you came Ivy. And you too, Elijah."

"Thank you for having us. All of you are so informal out here."

"We are, aren't we. I've no idea why. Maybe the people who came here before us just didn't have time for formalities. Just too busy trying to stay alive."

"How was your day at Taylor's today?" asked Bryan.

"Busy. I did manage to get two paintings done. Then spent the rest of the day taking photographs of all the plants that were shipping out today and tomorrow morning before I get there. People were still working when I left."

"And that's unusual?" asked Ivy.

"Shipping usually stopped around three to three-thirty, I think. But everyone's working overtime, trying to catch up."

"Why do they stop so early?" Ivy asked.

"Because they begin at seven, not long after sunup. And the shifts are probably only eight and half hours so there's no overtime."

"That early. Why?"

"I don't know. Maybe because nurseries are agricultural businesses. Farmers begin early. Watering to do. And the plants need to get to stores while they're still open and can be unloaded."

"Oh, that makes sense."

The garlic pizza was wonderful. Cheesy with their spicy red sauce. The rich flavor of Canadian bacon rose above all the other flavors, accented by the sweet intenseness of roasted red peppers, caramelized onions and roasted garlic. Divine.

Ivy seemed to be one of those very smart people who weren't entirely comfortable around others. Her conversation consisted of asking question after question. She also seemed to be trying to figure out the region and its inhabitants.

"So, there weren't any problems today?" asked Bryan, looking at her.

Gina said, "Not that I know of. Angie was there for a while. There were internet problems, but I don't think that's what you were asking about."

"No. Good to hear about Angie. And that there weren't any problems," he said.

Elijah had wolfed down his salad, four large slices of pizza and the soda.

"May I be excused. To go pet the cats?"

"Yes," said Ivy. "Go wash your hands first. The cats don't want tomato sauce on their beautiful clean fur.

Gina watched him with the cats. It wasn't long before Alice climbed in his lap and lay there purring loudly.

"I've never heard a cat purr so loud," said Ivy.

"Both of them do that. It's wonderful. Your son's been here at least an hour and hasn't once looked at a phone."

"He knows better. I'll take it away if he does."

"That's remarkable in this day and age."

"I know. He's really a good kid. He got bullied a lot in Chicago. It made him start skipping school to avoid them. He was taking the bus to the public library instead."

"Well, I hope it doesn't happen here. I know the schools put a lot of energy into anti-bullying campaigns."

"So far, so good," Ivy smiled.

"Are either of you coming any closer to catching someone for the problems at Taylor's?" asked Gina.

"Yes, we're coming closer, but not close enough yet," said Ivy.

"We've narrowed the field to less than ten," said Bryan.

"Good. I hope you narrow it to the person or people involved soon."

"Are people anxious?" he asked.

"They were on Saturday and yesterday. Probably today too. But at least there's no gas to explode anymore. No one said anything to me, but I know they'll all be relieved when things are wrapped up. Especially Cory."

"Are you going back tomorrow?" asked Bryan.

"Yes. Every day till Friday. It'll take me that long to photograph all the plants shipping out this week and during the weekend. And I have a meeting with Angie and Cory on Friday."

"Oh?" asked Bryan.

"I wanted to show them some paintings before I agreed to work there. And Cory has some plans he wants to talk to me about."

"It sounds like they're not only trying to catch up, but they're making changes too," said Bryan.

"You heard about the meeting yesterday."

"Just rumors," he said.

"Cory and Angie want to make the company worker owned. And go all in with solar or wind for their electricity. Plus make it a year-round operation, not just seasonal like it always has been. I think they're taking this opportunity to revolutionize the company and make it like I suspect they've always wanted to."

"And how do the workers feel about this?" asked Ivy.

"As far as I can tell, everyone loves it. I haven't hear anyone complain, but I'm sure there will be. People don't like change. But today everyone I saw seemed enthusiastic and excited. People were bustling about, trying to get things done. But I've only been there a week and not a day of it was normal, so I'm not a good judge."

Bryan nodded.

"I'll ask around," said Ivy. "Someone has pointed out that I need to talk to people more and be friendly. Not just show up when there's a problem." She looked at Bryan and smiled.

"That's not a bad idea. Talk to people about their kids. Ask about the schools. That would be some common ground," said Gina.

"How do you come up with ideas like that?" asked Ivy. "I have such a hard time with small talk."

"I used to be in retail. If you want to sell things without doing a hard-sell to people, you learn to do small talk. Compliment people on their hair, their purse, their shoes. Anything to break the ice," said Gina. "I used to ask them what they thought about a display I was working on. Were the earrings interesting or too gaudy? Did the colors work well together? I learned how to talk to people. Plus, I'm probably double your age. With age comes experience. And I don't have to care what people think of me anymore and can say whatever I please."

Ivy laughed, a deep rich sound that warmed the heart. Gina felt sure the woman never did that on the job.

"Sometimes I wish I could," said Bryan.

"Don't we all?" asked Ivy.

Bryan got up and collected all the dishes, taking them to the sink. He washed them and set put them in the drying rack.

"You don't have to do that," said Gina.

"But I'd like to," he said.

"Well okay then."

Ivy sat back in her chair. It was the most relaxed Gina had ever seen the woman.

"I think you need to give me lessons," she said.

"On what?"

"On how to talk to people."

"I could probably teach you some things, but really it's just an attitude."

"I need to learn that attitude if I'm going to do this job right. This isn't Chicago, where even in the same neighborhood, I rarely see the same person twice. Around here I keep running into the same people day after day."

"Well that's true. It's a small island and that's created a community. That's why I came here. Because it was so different than Seattle. Even though Capital Hill was a neighborhood, it wasn't a community. People had little in common and less time to get to know each other. There were so many distractions in the city," said Gina.

"How much should I pay you?" asked Ivy.

"I don't need money."

"I have to pay you something. What do you need?"

"Peace of mind. Solve this case. And you can take me out for tea and dessert."

"Done," said Ivy, holding out her hand. Gina shook it.

Bryan had finished the dishes and went to sit on the couch with Elijah. Alfred came over and sat on his lap.

"What a couple," said Ivy. "Men and cats. Why does the media never get that right? It's always the old cat lady."

"Misogyny I expect," said Gina. "Both women and cats have been reviled throughout the ages. So it's a convenient cliché."

Ivy looked startled.

"Didn't think I had an education, did you?" asked Gina, laughing.

"I don't associate artists with a knowledge of history, no."

"I like to surprise people. I love to learn and have always loved history. That's one of the reasons I began painting botanical art. I dabble at gardening, unlike my closest friend, who's a passionate gardener. And there's such a rich history in horticulture. All those plant hunters, past and present and their amazing adventures. And I'm painting plants they discovered or plants descended from their discoveries. I just love it."

"But I don't see many books here," said Ivy.

"C'mon," said Gina. She got up and led Ivy to the studio.

"If I keep them in here there's less cat hair to dust off. I don't allow the cats in this room. Plus there's more room in here."

She opened the door and they went inside. It was suitably messy for an artist. Piles of finished watercolors. The two unfinished washes. Paint tubes in a tray on the table. Brushes laid out to dry. A stack of plant books on another table. And a wall and a half of floor to ceiling book shelves, completely filled.

"There's another book shelf in the guest room. All the fiction. I keep everything in here that I might possibly need for painting."

"This is a wonderful space. Don't you get lonely working at home?"

"No. I'm quite contented sitting around painting. And when I've had enough of myself, I call someone up and go out to eat. I'm not that fond of cooking."

"It sounds like an ideal life. Do you have children?"

"Three daughters. One in the New York area who's married and trying to decide whether to keep making good money or have a baby, another in Los Angeles who makes masks for movies and the third is currently in China. She's the adventurer and travels as much as possible."

"Did you raise them alone?"

"No, I'm not as brave as you. My late husband, Ewan, helped a lot. It wasn't until they moved out and he retired that we moved here. Not long after that, he died. So I've been on my own for years."

"Do you miss him?"

"Sometimes. He was a good man, but he's been gone so long now that I've made a completely new life. One that I'm very happy with."

"And it's about to be completely upset again."

"Meaning?"

"Bryan."

"Oh, he told you. I don't know what will happen there. I don't know who he'll be after he retires and neither does he. Maybe we'll fit together or maybe not. Only time will tell."

"It's good you're not rushing into this, but from what I can tell the two of you are perfect for each other. I think he'll be really relieved to retire. I've seen a lot of cops burn out. He's getting close to that."

"I couldn't do your job. I can't imagine what it's like to do that year after year."

"I've always wanted to be a cop. My dad was and his dad. It's part of who I am. That desire to serve and do it well."

"You'd have to have that passion. I don't suppose it's an easy job for a woman in such a macho environment. Although this department doesn't feel macho to me, but I'd guess most are."

"Well my precinct was," said Ivy. "This one is much less so. I think Deputy Hammond has had a big effect on that. And Bryan."

"I don't think he has anything to prove."

"You're right. That's what it was in Chicago. Who was in charge, who was better than another, all that trash."

Alice streaked past them into the room and jumped up on Gina's reading chair.

"Alice, you know you can't be in here."

The cat ignored her and began to bathe.

"C'mon dear, out."

Gina lifted the cat and set her out in the hallway and Alice raced off down the hall like her tail was on fire.

Ivy came out of the studio and Gina shut the door.

"Well, we better get home. I'm sure Elijah has studying to do and I need to get some laundry done. Thank you so much for having us over with no notice. You are truly hospitable."

"You're welcome. It was lovely having both of you."

Gina followed Ivy back to the living room.

"Time to go Elijah. I know you've got studying."

"Okay," he said, lifting up Albert who was now on his lap and setting the cat on the couch. "Thank you for letting me play with your cats."

"You're very welcome. They haven't been getting enough attention lately. Thanks for giving them some."

He nodded.

Bryan handed Ivy one of the pizza boxes.

"No, I can't," she said.

"Yes, you can. I won't eat it. I'm working the next several days."

"Well, if you're sure."

"I'm sure," he said.

Ivy and Elijah thanked her again.

"I'll be calling you for that lesson and tea and dessert."

"I'll be waiting," said Gina.

They went out her front door and Gina closed it behind them.

"Suddenly, I'm very popular. Two people want to meet me for tea or coffee."

"Who else?" asked Bryan.

"Sandra Wells. Bob Taylor's ex."

"Cory and Angie's mother?"

"Yes. She's staying up here, to take care of Angie. I think she's afraid of getting lonely on Raven Island, amongst the illiterati."

"Well, that's interesting."

"Surely she's not a suspect."

"No, she's not. I just didn't know she was staying. She is on the board, although I'm not sure why."

"She has enough money to invest in films. Maybe she invested in Taylor Gardens."

"Maybe. I put several pieces of pizza in your fridge. Thought you might want it for lunches."

"Oh thank you. I'm getting tired of sandwiches. But are you sure you don't want any?"

"No. I really won't eat it. The days I'm on duty I like to go out to eat. It's just easier."

"Okay."

"I hope it was all right that I brought them over. Corvid's was filled with high school kids celebrating something. They really wouldn't have gotten in before closing."

"It was just fine. I had a good time talking to Ivy and her son is delightful."

"He is, isn't he? He seems like a really great kid. A little lost, but I think he'll find his way. Well, I better get going. I've got an early morning tomorrow and you probably do too."

Gina sighed.

"Yes, I've got to take photos of several days' worth of

shipping. Same on Wednesday. Because they're going to be shipping out all weekend as well as mornings before I get there and afternoons after I leave. I figured it'll take me two full days of taking photos just to get half a day ahead. Then I can take pictures and paint on Thursday. This is turning out to be more work than I anticipated and it sounds like Cory wants to give me even more work."

"Like what?"

"When they go to worker owned, they'll add in fall and winter plants. So two extra seasons of plant tags to paint. Plus, he's got something he wants to talk to me about on Friday. No idea what, he seemed reluctant to talk about it in passing. Which suggests to me that it's a huge project and he wants to have the time to convince me to do it."

"Do you want to add in more work?"

"I don't know. I'm enjoying it, well except for the murder and things. And next year it wouldn't be as much work. I'll only need to paint new introductions. I guess I'll just wait and see what he has in mind."

"When are you meeting on Friday."

"Morning sometime. Why?"

"I don't know. I'll need to make a few unscheduled trips through this week. Just to check on things and see if anything shakes loose."

"So you think the person works at Taylor's?"

"Can't answer that."

"Of course."

"No, I mean I'm not a hundred percent sure who it is. Yet. But we're getting closer."

"Good."

"Well, I will say goodnight now. Or I'll be here all night."

He gave her a kiss on the forehead and left through the front door.

"Don't forget to lock up," he said, before closing it.

She locked the front door knowing he was waiting to hear the lock click. She always locked the door, since she rarely used it.

It was almost ten. She should get to bed.

What exactly did he expect to shake loose by his showing up at Taylor Gardens?

GINA SAT IN ONE OF THE NEW TRAILERS THAT HAD BEEN delivered that morning. To create enough space for everyone on shift, it took two trailers for the break rooms.

The trailers had been filled with new plastic tables and chairs, bought online and delivered by Costco that morning. How had Emily or Carla gotten them to deliver way out here? The closest store was half an hour away. Maybe because of the bulk order. Wholesale prices might have been cheaper elsewhere but being able to get things so quickly was probably worth paying extra.

Each trailer had been fitted out with a new refrigerator and microwave. The windows had been opened to bring in fresh air and rid the room of the new plastic smell which combined badly with the scent of everyone's combined lunches and sweaty bodies.

Gina had brought leftover pizza, which only added to the smell. She'd just finished eating and leaned back in the folding chair, sipping her jasmine iced tea, while listening to Shawna and David talk about how Shawna could work through the fall with a baby.

She felt tired. She'd photographed countless plants all morning. Each plant Gina found had five or six varieties. Different colors or patterns of flowers. Some had more. There were seventeen distinct petunia varieties. Some of them were stunning. One was hot pink with white spots. It almost made her want to put them into a container with plants equally as gaudy.

Almost. She needed to hold firm with her no container rule or spend all summer fussing with it and watering.

She'd made good progress on checking photographed plants off the shipping list. But there were still hundreds more to capture in the next couple of days. Plants were leaving the shipping area at blindly fast rates. All those extra hours were paying off.

Cory had announced in the morning that if all went well today and tomorrow, they'd be back on schedule. Which made everyone very excited. It seemed to spur people on to work even more steadily.

Last week there'd been a lot of times when she saw people standing around discussing things. This week everyone had their heads down and was working hard. Was it because they were behind or because in a few months they'd be part owners of the company? Everyone would have skin in the game now.

"What do you think, Gina?" asked David.

"I'm sorry, I was wool-gathering and not listening. What do I think about what?"

"The worker-owned thing that Cory's planning," said Shawna.

"I think it's great. If I worked here full time, I'd be excited to own a stake in Taylor Gardens. I think it will make people more responsible. Most of them anyway. Why?"

"Some people don't want to be part of it," said David.

"Why?"

"They don't want that responsibility. They want to go on as they always have. They're happy only working six months a year. Others just don't think it will work. And some think it'll just be extra work and they won't get anything back," said Shawna.

David nodded his head.

"Well, they could be right, but I don't think so. I think Cory and Angie will make sure it's fair. They *are* asking people to be on the committee. I think they'll listen to what folks want to do. This company has been successful for a long time and I think they're making the right changes for the future. I think being environmentally conscious, besides being trendy, is the ethical way to go. I believe in taking the high road. It doesn't always bring immediate results, but long term it's a better choice."

"I agree," said Shawna. "I just worry about changing so much, so fast."

"If not everyone wants change," said David, "maybe those people can continue to be seasonal workers. I bet we'll still have more work in late winter and spring than the other seasons. They could opt out of being an owner."

"That's a good idea," said Shawna. "You should so sign up to be on that committee. You always think outside the box."

"Thanks," said David. "Maybe I will."

"I'd better get back to taking photographs," said Gina. "Before those plants are gone."

"Make sure you take breaks," said Shawna.

"I will. I brought my chair. I think I'll drag it along with me this afternoon. I can take photos sitting down."

"Good," said David. "Can't exhaust our only artist."

"Thanks for looking out for me," said Gina.

She got up and took the lunch bag out to her car. Dragged her camp chair out of the back seat. Carrying only her chair and water bottle, she set off.

An hour later, she was in the middle of photographing twenty different varieties of *Osteospermum*. African daisies came in the most beguiling shades. One of her new favorites, *Osteospermum 'Purple Sun'* had petals that were a medium purple on the inside edges which blended to salmon in the middle with tips in a cadmium yellow-orange. The way the colors faded into each other made the flowers glow.

She'd always loved African daisies, despite their continual need for deadheading. Not enough to buy them. Although she might pick up one of these at the store. Tuck it into a sunny area of the garden for some seasonal complexity.

A shadow fell over her and she looked up. It was Sheriff Jannson.

"Oh hello," she said, taking the photo and then standing up. Her knees creaked as she rose.

"Good afternoon. How's things."

"Quiet, but busy."

"I've noticed. I've been looking for Cory for an hour. He's always on the move. By the time I get to where he was, he's gone."

"I haven't even seen him today. Although I have been concentrating on getting photos taken."

"How long will you be here today?"

Gina glanced at her phone.

"I think my battery's good for another hour. Then, I'll go home and recharge it. I probably need a new phone. This one doesn't hold its charge long, anymore. The new car came first."

"Good choice."

"Why do you ask?"

"I just wanted to know."

"Are you keeping tabs on me?" she asked.

"Yeah, I guess I am. I just feel better knowing where you are. Because of the situation. Does that bother you?"

"No. Not in the circumstances. If you were doing it when I was out and about in my daily life, I might. I don't know. Check back in a few months," she laughed.

"Good. I promise I'm not a control freak in my personal life. I'm not that guy."

"Good thing," she said.

"Well, I'll move along. Don't want to let folks around here get the right impression. I don't want to make you a target."

"Got it. May your shaking things up have the desired effect," said Gina, smiling.

She continued taking photos until her battery dropped to five percent. Time to pack it in. She'd gotten everything checked off her list for today and two more plants that she'd scheduled for tomorrow. Whew.

Gina sat for a moment, looking at the *Ageratum* she'd been taking photos of. Low growing plants with fluffy flower in purples, pinks and white. She didn't ask it of many plants, but what was the point of them?

They were uninteresting. Their flowers too small to make the soft spiky petals visible. They were little puffs of color and boring colors at that. Even if she put together containers or baskets, they were a plant that she'd never use.

She sipped some water from her bottle. Still cold and refreshing. Time to go.

Gina returned the small pots to their places. Then put the list, pen and phone into the vest pocket, zipping them inside. She folded up her chair and picked up the water bottle.

Taking the chair to her car, she breathed in the warmish fresh spring air, feeling a sense of ease. Summer was coming.

Then she went to the office trailer. Angie, Mckenzie and Cory were the only ones there, clearly having a meeting.

Gina signed out, waving to them. They waved back but continued their discussion. Something about money and priorities. She left the trailer and walked back to her car.

Had the insurance given them an estimate of what they'd pay for? Angie was clearly itching to buy those solar panels. And they needed to rebuild greenhouses and shipping. They'd also need a new break room and office. It must be costing a fair amount to rent the three trailers.

At home Gina plugged in her phone as the cats rubbed against her legs.

"Just because I'm home doesn't mean it's dinnertime. I'm home early," she said, petting them.

She took her shoes and socks off and went barefoot. Gina considered dealing with the piles of mail that had come in. Then decided to do it on the weekend when she'd have time to pay bills. She quickly recycled things that were obviously junk and piled the bills together.

Enough work for today. She looked in the fridge to consider dinner options. Leftover pizza and some chicken pasta with an Alfredo sauce, that she'd taken out of the freezer a couple of days ago. There were enough leftovers so she didn't need to cook for three more nights. But on Friday, she should probably go buy some groceries. After the meeting Friday morning.

Gina went into her studio and looked at the paintings. She had a few. Enough for the meeting.

There was only one she wasn't completely happy with, but it was good enough. She simply wasn't enamored of grape hyacinths. The problem wasn't the painting, it was her.

She'd also done the paintings in three different styles, from fuzzy to more detailed. She suspected they'd want more detailed paintings to represent the individual plants, although the fuzzier ones captured the feeling of the plants in the landscape better.

Gina felt too tired to paint today. She'd been so focused on the visual all day. She needed to do something else for a while.

A hot bath would be just the thing. Gina poured lavender bath salts into the tub, lit a lemongrass candle and luxuriated in the hot water. Sinking down into it up to her chin. Her late husband, Ewan, had been right to have the bathroom remodeled before they moved in, with a long deep tub.

The heat loosened all her sore and tired muscles. She'd done a lot of squatting down this morning to photograph plants at eye level. Maybe she could bring the light metal rolling cart that was in her studio tomorrow. That would lift the plants up higher and make them easier to shoot. She'd have to think about whether it was worth the trouble.

Her thoughts wandered back through the day. Who had Shawna been talking about when she'd said people didn't think the worker-owned piece wouldn't work? And who just wanted things to go on as they always had?

Was one of those people behind the murder?

She heard her phone ring in the kitchen. No way was she going to race through the house trying to answer it. Whoever it was would have to wait. No one was going to have an emergency while she was taking a bath.

She should probably call her daughters. Check in and see what they were up to. Maybe on the weekend.

Perhaps by then, the person behind all this mess would be arrested and she could set it aside. She was definitely *not* going to tell her daughters about it.

When the murders had happened at Ravenswood, Joanna and Trina had demanded she retire. And stay home in safety. Shelley had been worried, but only demanded that she call once a week. Shelley was the traveler and understood that the world wasn't always safe.

So Gina had decided they simply didn't need to know about certain things. She'd talk about her painting and Melanie. Her garden and the cats. She hadn't told any of them about Bryan, mostly because there really wasn't anything to tell yet. When they began to date regularly, then she'd tell them.

After her bath, Gina dressed in soft cotton pajamas. She fluffed up her hair and let it dry on its own.

She really should flatten those paintings before Friday. She could probably get three done tonight and then the rest done tomorrow and Thursday.

Gina went into the studio and cleared a space on the table. She plugged in the clothes iron and turned it to cotton. Then pulled out the old cotton sheet, folding it in half. Putting the first painting face down between two layers of the sheet, she ironed it smooth. Then turned the iron off and lay a drawing board over the sheet, piling it high with heavy books to weigh everything down. Then she left the painting to cool.

Out in the kitchen, Gina remembered the phone call. She didn't recognize the number, although it was local. There was no message.

She decided on pasta for dinner but fed the circling sharks first. Otherwise they'd never leave her alone. Then she spooned some pasta on a plate and put it in the microwave to heat.

There was a knock at her door. Gina peered out the peephole. Sheriff Winters stood there.

Gina opened the door.

"Hello," she said, "come in."

"I can't. I just wanted a quick word."

"Come in quickly. Cats."

"Oh, I forgot," said the sheriff, stepping inside the door. Gina closed it.

"What can I do for you?"

"I just wanted to make sure you're okay. I called from the office, but there was no answer. I thought you kept your cell phone with you."

"I do, but I was taking a bath. And my battery was nearly dead, so I wanted to charge it up."

"Oh, good. I'm glad. I just wanted to check in and make sure you were all right."

"Why wouldn't I be?"

"I know Sheriff Jannson said he was going to be riling things up today at Taylor Gardens. I just wanted to make sure you weren't in the middle of it."

"Did something else happen?"

"Not yet. But it will. You sure you want to be there this week?"

"I really do need to finish taking photos. Plants are shipping out so fast."

"Okay. Well, keep your eyes open and if things don't feel right, get out. Fast."

"Thank you," said Gina. "I appreciate your looking out for me."

"Well if you get hurt, I'll have to wait longer for those lessons."

Gina laughed.

"Okay, I'm off to go pick up Elijah. And it smells like you've got dinner to eat. I'll check in again sometime tomorrow."

"I probably won't be in the bath. Although my battery might be just as dead."

"Don't let it get that far. You might need the phone."

"It just goes down so fast when I'm taking photos."

"Always leave yourself at least ten percent. Be safe please."

"All right. Tomorrow I'll quit at ten percent no matter what. Promise."

"Good. See you," said the sheriff, opening the door and closing it behind her.

Gina locked the door and went back into the kitchen.

They must be expecting something big to happen and soon. For both of them to warn her.

She ate dinner looking out over her garden and the sliver of a view she had that lay beyond it. The clouds began to color up with salmon, hot pink and a purple-gray color. The cats sat silhouetted on the windowsill, bathing.

After dinner, she got two more paintings flattened. In between, she read through the new watercolor magazine that had come. There were two interesting techniques she wanted to try out and one of the paint companies she bought from had some new iridescent colors coming out that were interesting. They might be fun to play with.

She watched some mindless television and went to bed early. Tomorrow would be another busy day.

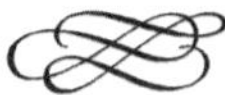

Gina arrived at 7:30 a.m. to sign in. Emily, Carla and Angie were all busily working at computers, so she just signed in, waved and went about her work.

She'd decided against the rolling cart and just planned to stretch out more. People were beginning to look tired. This was the third day of most of them working overtime. With one more day in sight.

That was in addition to all the stress of the previous week. Halfway through the morning, Mckenzie found her and handed Gina a new sheet of paper.

"This is an update of what's shipping out today and the next two days. Some changes have been made. Without heat, some plants have been moved up, others pushed back. Some aren't filling out as fast as they would with heat."

"Thank you," said Gina.

"Have you seen Cory?"

"Not in a couple of days."

"He's crazy busy right now. Well, if you see him, I'm looking for him. I'll do a quick check around and then go back to the computer. I can't get him on his phone cause he left that in the office. Which means he's completely overwhelmed. That's the only time he does forgetful stuff like that."

"I can't imagine all the things he's trying to juggle."

"I can. And I wouldn't do it. Well, I'm off to search for him."

Gina sat in her chair and looked at the new list, comparing it to the old one and checking off the plants she'd already photographed. Yesterday, she'd gotten all the plants that were shipping out today, except one group that had been added into a late afternoon shipment. She'd do those first and then work on what was shipping out tomorrow morning.

The new list didn't have the greenhouses marked on them. Gina transferred the greenhouse numbers to the new list, hoping plants hadn't been moved.

She set off to find the columbine. They were in the greenhouse listed. There were purple and white ones, red and white, clear bright white and a dark purple one that looked nearly black. As well as a yellow and red one that resembled the *Aquilegia* native to the region, but this one was a hybrid and much larger. She photographed them all quickly.

Then moved on to searching for *Heuchera*. Coral bells, a perennial, had become hugely popular in the gardening community over the last decade. New varieties with stunning foliage had been bred and developed. Gina had several in her garden. Some did better in shade, others in sun. They were grown mainly for their mounding decorative foliage, the flowers were tiny bells held on foot-tall stalks. The foliage was more colorful. The leaves came in shades of purple, coral, green and amber and were often variegated or heavily patterned.

Gina picked out one of each of the ten varieties that she found. She recognized the breeder's name. They were the source of many new introductions. Probably, next year there would be different hot new ones, but she'd paint these, just in case some of them were returning.

She'd photographed two when she heard Cory's voice. Standing up, she saw him coming into the greenhouse.

"Gina, how's it going?" he asked.

"Good. I'm keeping ahead of the schedule, at least."

"Good. How many paintings will you have for Friday?"

"Maybe eight, we'll see. Depends on how tomorrow goes. I'm just photographing today. And yesterday. Things are shipping out too fast to do any painting."

"Eight's plenty. Don't stress yourself about it. There's too much stress around here already."

"About what? I thought things were going well."

"Shipping out plants is going wonderfully. Everyone's going the extra mile." Cory looked around and then lowered his voice. "It's the other changes. Not everyone's happy about our idea to be worker-owned. I thought people would be thrilled about it. But change is hard."

"Who's not happy?"

"I don't know who all isn't. The thing I keep hearing is 'Jason said this might happen.' Or 'Jason said there will be more overtime, but we won't get paid for it.' So it might just be Jason who's at the heart of it."

"Can't you just fire him?"

"Not without good cause. He hasn't given me the cause, either. He makes nice to me, just like he did to Dad. Then talks badly behind my back. He's a piece of work. I don't know what to do with him. I wish he'd come to talk to me instead of spreading false rumors."

"People like him can ruin a workplace. I've seen it happen."

"I know. I just haven't come up with a solution yet. I know he's pissed because Dad promoted us kids over him. What did he expect in a family-owned business? Angie and I paid our way through college to learn more about business and came back here to work. We've been working our tails off ever since. Dustin did too, even though he played a lot. He had good plans."

"I wish I had some ideas for you. Perhaps suggest if he doesn't want to be part of a worker-owned business, there are plenty others to choose from?" asked Gina.

"I don't know what I'm going to do. But I'll need to come up with something and soon. He's spreading a lot of bad vibes. I figure I'll try to tackle it on Friday. Have a quick meeting where I spread some good vibes. We'll be past the craziness of trying to get back on track by then. I should have most of the news about when we can begin rebuilding."

"Have you got the insurance money already?"

"No, not yet, but it should be soon. And even if I have to remortgage my house and Dad's, we'll get the money. Mother's offered financial help if we need it too. We've gotta get started on things. Construction always takes longer than you think it does."

"That's always been my experience," said Gina.

"Well, I'm going back to the office."

"Oh, Mckenzie's looking for you. She said she'll be in the office. Where your phone is."

Cory patted his back pocket.

"Oh. Didn't know I'd forgotten it. Wondered why it was so quiet and no one had called or texted." He laughed and left the greenhouse.

Gina smiled. She finished with the *Heuchera*. She'd need to pick up one of the varieties.

Heuchera 'Topaz Jazz' was a lovely butterscotch color with heavily-veined palmate leaves. The leaves varied in color, probably from sunlight and temperature. They ranged between a pale-greenish to a pinkish-red. Each plant had a combination of leaves in all colors. The flowers, instead of the normal pinkish color were a surprising rich butter yellow. She loved that one and knew just where to put it.

Gina returned the plants to the places she'd found them, collapsed her chair and moved on to the next ones on the list. By lunchtime, she'd done half the list. Her battery was at fifty percent.

At lunch she put her bag down on the table Mckenzie and Shawna were at. David had forgotten his lunch and run into town to pick up a burger somewhere. Gina pulled out the plastic bag containing leftover pizza and set the slices on a paper towel in the microwave.

When she returned to the table, Shawna had been talking quietly with Mckenzie and stopped when Gina sat down.

"Am I interrupting something?" Gina asked.

"No, I just feel guilty gossiping," said Shawna.

"Don't stop on my account," said Gina. "I might've done it a few times. Better to vent than let things stew."

She didn't really mean it, just wanted to put Shawna at ease. And the more gossip she heard, the better she'd be able to help the Sheriffs.

"Well, Jason's been talking a lot. Complaining to anyone

who will listen. He floats from team to team, he's been taking Angie's place since she can't be there. Anyway, because he floats, he's talking to everyone. About how the worker-owned thing is a bad idea. He's come up with every bad thing under the sun that could possibly happen. And quite a few that couldn't. And he's just spreading lies and bad feelings."

"Is he doing anything that could get him fired," asked Mckenzie.

"No, he's too smart for that. Unfortunately. I used to think he was a good guy. But all this lying and bad-mouthing Cory and Angie just makes me mad."

"I can imagine," said Gina. "Do people believe him?"

"Some of them. Some of them see right through him, I think. But too many of them are afraid of the things he's telling them happening. The newer people, who don't know Cory and Angie as well. I don't know any way of dealing with it. I'm only on one team and I only hear it then. He's my superior, so I don't tell him off to his face. I wait till he's floated and tell the others he's just talking trash. He's a bitter old man who hides it well."

Mckenzie said, "And then there's John. He's even worse."

"Who's John?" asked Gina, quietly.

"He's the Shipping Head. Tall and skinny with glasses. He was injured slightly in the blast. The force of it threw him into a greenhouse post and broke his glasses. He came through fine though. Just a few scratches from flying greenhouse glass. He has new glasses now."

"Oh, I remember seeing him. What's he doing?"

"Complaining even worse. He's really pissed off about all the overtime. He's sort of required to do it, being Shipping Head. Plants are moving out at a good rate, but because he's angry all the time it's an awful place to be. He spends his time yelling at everyone about how slow they are. People just want to transfer to a different team or quit. Cory's had to talk two people down and switch three others out of shipping. Everyone hates him," said Mckenzie.

"I had no idea," said Gina. "I'm off in my own little world."

"It's good you're missing all this," said Shawna. "I wouldn't wish it on anyone."

Gina ate her leftover pizza, enjoying the intense cheeses, the rich Canadian bacon and the wonderful garlic flavor.

Talk turned to the open house in June. Mckenzie was trying to firm up the catering menu for the plant breeders and other industry reps who would be coming.

"I've got smoked salmon crostini, tapenade crostini, grilled asparagus, green salad with wild greens, avocado, tomatoes and balsamic vinegar and olive oil dressing. Plus, mini strawberry tarts for dessert. What should we have to drink?"

"Alcohol or not?" asked Gina.

"No alcohol. We'd need a license and it's just too complicated," said Mckenzie.

"Water, iced tea and lemonade?" said Gina.

"Oh, I didn't think of iced tea. We could get bottled iced teas and water. Perhaps get the caterers to make real lemonade."

"If you want to go exotic, lavender lemonade," said Shawna.

"Oh, I love lavender lemonade," said Gina.

"I've never had it. Will it go with the food?" asked Mckenzie.

"I don't think lavender lemonade would," said Gina. "But

some plant people would love it anyway. It would go with dessert."

"I'll ask the caterers. Good. I need another vegetable salad, I'll need to ask them about that too," said Mckenzie. "Have to have this menu nailed by Monday."

"Well good. You're ahead of things," said Gina. "And how are you doing with all this overtime," she asked Shawna.

"I'm not doing all of it. My feet get too swollen. Cory told me to go home when I need to."

"Good. Well, I'd better get back to work so I can finish before my phone battery dies. It's going to be a race."

"How old is your phone?" asked Shawna.

"Ancient. And long overdue for replacement. I should have money in June for a new one. Maybe earlier, we'll see." Gina took her lunch bag out to the car.

In the parking lot she spotted John. He stood mostly behind an old white pickup and was talking to another worker whose face she couldn't see.

John was shouting, "I hate him! It should have worked!"

Gina pretended she didn't see or hear them, while listening intently and putting her lunch bag in the car and pulling her chair back out. She locked her car and slowly closed the door but heard nothing more.

She glanced back in that direction while turning to go to the greenhouses. They were either gone or had hidden.

Who was the other worker? They'd both had short dark hair. Probably a man. Most of the women had longer hair. Gina tried to remember if they were tall or short? Shorter than John, so probably normal height. Average build and wearing a company t-shirt, like many of the workers.

Gina continued on to the greenhouse with the next plants

she needed to photograph. In the other half of the greenhouse a team of workers were moving out plants.

She walked among the Rex *Begonia*. Their showy leaves spiraled out around the circumference of the plant. Each leaf was a masterpiece of markings. Patterns in colors red, purple, green, mint and chartreuse. Some had a hairy texture, others smooth. Each variety was unique and stunning. Too bad they weren't hardy around here.

If she was one for houseplants, Gina would have grown these. They were beautiful. But she'd sworn off houseplants, except for two, easy to care for, Christmas cactus. The cats seemed to leave those alone.

She picked one each of the ten different varieties and set to work taking photos. In the time it had taken her to choose plants, the team across the main walkway had their side of the greenhouse half-emptied. They were working so fast.

Gina took the photos, remembering to stretch out as she returned each plant to its spot. By the time she'd finished, Gina had talked herself into the possibility of one more houseplant. She could put it in the studio where the cats couldn't reach it.

She sat down in her chair and perused the list for the next plants just as the crew finished clearing the other half of the greenhouse. They whooped and wheeled out the rolling shelves laden with petunias.

Sheriff Jannson strolled down the walkway past them.

"Well hello. Glad to see you're taking it easy," he said.

"Funny," she said. "And what brings you to my humble throne?"

"Just needed a walk. It gets tiring driving that big SUV around. Needed to stretch my legs."

"I've got some things to share with you."

"Oh?"

She told him about what she'd learned that day, from Cory, and then the conversation with Shawna and Mckenzie. Then described what she'd seen in the parking lot.

"Good work," he said. "That helps a lot, thanks. I want you to continue to keep your eyes and ears open. Mainly for your own safety. I've set some things in motion and there will be fallout. So be careful who you're hanging out with and where."

"Anyone I should avoid?"

"Cory and Angie. They're the most likely targets still. I'd stay out of shipping too."

"I have no reason to be there. But I have a meeting with Cory and Angie on Friday morning."

"Just don't linger, okay? Where's the meeting?"

"The office trailer."

"Okay. I'll make sure I'm nearby. Just in case. I don't know what will happen. But we've got to flush out the person behind this."

"Behind this? Then there's more than one."

"I don't have all the information yet. I think there are one, maybe two people, besides Carlos. Maybe more. We'll find out."

"Okay. I'll try to stay safe."

"Don't just try. Do. Please."

She nodded.

"I'll move on now. See you later."

"Bye."

Gina hurried through the rest of the afternoon. Not only because she felt uneasy, but because the phone battery was nearly gone. It was as if she believed taking photos quickly would use less battery. But it was probably all the turning on and off that was doing it.

By four her battery was at nine percent, but she'd finished today's photos. Gina loaded up her car and signed out. The only person in the office was Carla. They waved at each other and Gina went to her car.

She was on her way home, when the thought of leftover pasta came to her. It sounded awful. So she went to Corr's instead. And wandered the aisles before settling on some frozen cheese enchiladas. She bought a couple other frozen dinners and some bread. That should take her through till the weekend. She passed on the chocolate cake, feeling very proud of herself.

At home she fed the cats and microwaved her dinner. She flipped through the uninteresting mail. Then found a postcard of Yuyuan gardens from Shelly. She was in Shanghai. The note read:

Hi Mom,

You'd love this garden. Amazing rocks. Wish you were here. Will write a real letter soon.

Love,

Shel

That was sweet. Gina stuck the postcard to her refrigerator next to the dozen or so already there. All from Shelley. Her other daughters rarely traveled. Or if they did, they didn't send postcards.

Gina spent the evening flattening more paintings and relaxing. She went to bed early again. Tomorrow she'd take photos in the morning and get to paint in the afternoon. Maybe she'd come home and do it. Maybe not. She'd see how things felt.

It felt good to be a few days ahead of shipping at least.

Thoughts of the discussions throughout her day threatened to keep her awake. She pushed them out of her mind and fell asleep. But the worries returned, causing disturbing dreams.

THURSDAY MORNING

GINA DRAGGED HERSELF OUT OF BED, EXHAUSTED. BY THE TIME she'd gotten two cups of extra-strong black tea, breakfast and dressed, it was eight. She hurried to get ready, deciding to leave her paint supplies at home.

She was too tired. She'd just take photos and come home. Maybe paint, maybe not. She did pack a lunch, just in case taking the photos ran into the afternoon.

No one was in the office when she arrived. Gina signed in and went to the greenhouses, looking for the plants she needed. Everyone seemed to be gathered in the courtyard. She walked out to find out what was going on, carrying her chair and a small bag with her lunch and water.

Cory was standing off to one side with Angie, Mckenzie and Emily. He was talking.

"Now I know many of you have been speculating on what might happen with this company. There's a lot of rumors going around and the ones I've heard are all wrong.

"You may think I'd be angry and you're right. Many of you

have known me for years. I used to work in the greenhouses, right alongside you. But I don't care if you think badly of me. What really makes me furious is that all of you here have been working alongside Angie all this time. You should all know that she wouldn't allow me to say okay to a plan that took advantage of any of you. She'd kick me all the way to the middle of the Pacific and let me drown first.

"I don't have answers to you about the details of the worker-owned plans because they haven't been made yet. Several people have signed up for the committee. We haven't met yet. Many of you might remember that Angie and I just buried our brother five days ago. We're still grieving even if we're here at work. And Angie just got out of the hospital. She's still far from a hundred percent. Plus, we've been trying to keep this business running so it can stay alive and all of us can get paid. I've got kids to support too and they like to eat.

"I wish I could tell you I've got a huge savings account, but my family is living paycheck to paycheck just like many of yours. All my extra money has gone back into this company. For years. Long before I became management. And Angie's done the same. Those new chairs in the break room last year? They were from me. The walkie talkies those of you out in the field wear to ask questions and save some steps, those were from Angie. She would've bought the solar panels too, but she likes to eat. We've done things like that stealthily, cause Dad didn't approve. He wanted us to have money. And my wife gets annoyed when she can't buy our daughter new school clothes or help our sons out with tuition, cause I spent the money on new computers for the office because our old ones were breaking down. But enough about us.

"Taylor's is doing great by the way. I appreciate the

immense hard work all of you have put in during the last few days to make it happen. We'll be back on schedule before the day ends. That's nothing short of a miracle. I don't have news about reconstruction yet. We're still talking to the insurance company and doing new paperwork they send over as fast as it comes in the door. We may need to borrow money to get repairs moving more quickly, but it'll happen.

"What is not helping is people complaining and speculating on everything that might possibly go wrong in the future. It just makes everyone feel bad and doesn't solve any real problems. If you've got a problem, come to me to complain. I'll listen. If someone's complaining to you, tell them to be quiet. If they won't, talk to a supervisor. If it's a supervisor complaining, come talk to me. Or Angie.

"We're not going to let this fester like an infected wound. We all have enough drama to deal with during the peak shipping season. Let's not make more. Let's prop each other up and help everyone feel better. We're a community here. Let's act like one. If you don't feel you can be part of this, then let me, Angie, or Emily know. The time to walk away is now. You don't even have to give two weeks' notice. Just leave an address we can mail your check to. We'll pay you for those two weeks and any vacation time that's owed you. I don't want people here who don't want to be here. Now, I've got phone calls to make. If anyone wants to talk to me, I'll be in the office. Thanks for listening."

With that Cory walked towards the office. His face was red and he looked like he was barely containing the fury.

Gina hoped that people had the sense to wait for him to cool down before going and asking questions. She looked around. People looked shocked. She'd bet a good pair of shoes that no one knew about him and Angie funneling their earnings back into the company. Even Mckenzie had looked stunned when he'd said that.

Some of the workers looked guilty. Others looked angry, although Gina couldn't tell what about. John stood off to one side, his expression blank. She looked for Jason and found him in a group of men, talking quietly. He looked like he was trying to convince them of something.

Shawna came up beside Gina.

"Good morning. I'm completely ashamed of every bad thought I've ever had about Cory or Angie. Wow. Can you believe they did that?"

"Yes, I can. I haven't known many people who would, but there are more of them than we think in the world. You couldn't have had many bad thoughts."

"Oh you know how it is, when your hormones are raging and everything's looking bleak and then one of them comes along while I'm working hard and feeling put upon and they say, 'There's mandatory overtime tomorrow.' That's enough to set me off."

"Oh, those sorts of thoughts. Well, we all have them. Especially when the hormones are raging. I can imagine yours have been on a roller coaster lately."

"Oh yeah. Does it end?"

"Yes, but you've got a lot of years till then. It took me ten years of going through menopause, which is common I hear. Everything got worse. Super heavy periods, raging emotions, sleep deprivation. And that was after three pregnancies and raising my daughters. Then all that turmoil just faded away with my periods. And now, I can count on my mind being clear and my body, while it's falling apart from aging, I pretty much know what it's going to do. It's actually quite wonderful to feel like I know things and am strong and powerful. Except when I'm too tired."

"Awesome. I'll bet you don't miss the turmoil."

"I don't. I love my life. I'm lucky. I'm financially stable and I have friends and cats."

"Do you miss your husband?"

"Sometimes, but he's been gone a long time."

"So no boyfriend."

"There might be one. We'll see how things develop."

"Do I know him?"

"I don't know," asked Gina. "I'll tell you his name if and when it becomes a going concern."

"We could double date. Or if it takes too long, triple date. Or no, I guess it would be a double date plus one. I am so not having twins." Shawna laughed.

Gina laughed, too.

"Well, I'd better get to work. I'm looking forward to being caught up today. And life returning to just the normal busy," said Shawna.

"Me too. I've gotta get photos of plants leaving this weekend and Monday morning's shipments. I'm a bit ahead. Then, I can begin painting again."

They began walking to the greenhouse.

"Can't you just take all the photos at once?"

"Then I'd be photographing plants with buds, not blossoms. I want them at their peak. Some of them I've never seen in bloom. And others have a dozen or more varieties. Petunias."

"I know. We sort of went crazy with petunias this year. So

many new ones. Cool patterns and a lot of them are self-cleaning."

"Self-cleaning? What does that mean?"

"The dead blooms fall off and the plant keeps throwing out buds. No deadheading needed by the customer."

"That's wonderful. It's almost enough to make me want to do a container or two. Almost."

"Why wouldn't you?" asked Shawna.

"Watering."

"There is that. You could put them on a drip system that's separate for your garden, so you could run it every day or two."

Gina laughed.

"Too much maintenance for me. My garden's enough. But I'm going to hunt down one of those Topaz Jazz *Heuchera* for the garden."

"Oh, those are pretty."

Gina had stopped by a group of *Gazania*.

"Well, this is my first stop for the day. I'll see you later," she said.

Shawna waved and continued on to another greenhouse.

Gina set up her chair and left her small bag on it. She took photos of the *Gazania rigens*. They were planted in two-gallon tan plastic pots. Each pot held three large plants. They were just coming into bloom and most pots contained plants with all the different flower markings and colors.

The solid flowers came in white, yellow, orange and a pale purplish-pink color, but most of the blooms had a vibrant contrasting stripe that ran the length of each petal. These were also called African daisies, just like the *Osteosperum* which she'd already photographed. They were two different, but similar plants. Which was the problem with common names for plants. The Latin names were more precise, even though it meant taking the time to learn new names for everything.

Gina loved these bright little pots full of spring color. They'd bloom all summer long if someone picked the dead flowers off and continued to water them occasionally. She knew from experience that the flowers closed at night and opened with the sun. On dark cloudy days, they simply remained closed. They obviously hadn't evolved to live in the Pacific Northwest.

She took many photos of the different combinations, even though there would be one tag for all of them. The customer had to see them in bloom to get a combination of colors they wanted. Most people probably didn't care. They just wanted the splash of color.

Each flower was amazingly complex. Had the stripe originally evolved to create a visual path for pollinators? Many plants did that. Or perhaps it had been a fluke in some greenhouse that humans took advantage of.

She moved on to the next plants. There seemed to be less chatter in the greenhouse this morning. Everyone had their head down working.

By lunchtime, Gina was nearly finished with her list for the day. She didn't feel exhausted, but there still probably wouldn't be any painting today. She'd iron the last couple of paintings and get everything organized for tomorrow's meeting.

She ate lunch with Emily and Mckenzie.

"So, three people quit this morning," said Emily.

"Who?" asked Mckenzie.

"I'm probably not supposed to talk about it, but it'll

become obvious, won't it? Jason quit, along with Trang and Chris," said Emily.

"I'm glad Jason quit," said Mckenzie. "He was really making Cory crazy. But what about John?"

"Nope. I hear he's still making everyone's lives in shipping a living hell."

"Too bad," said Mckenzie.

Gina ate her melted cheddar and tomato sandwich, enjoying the richness of the sharp cheddar.

She felt relieved Jason was gone. He'd been making so many people dissatisfied with their jobs. John didn't seem much better, spreading chaos in his own way.

"Hey, we should have a baby shower for Shawna," said David, coming to sit down at the table.

"Oh, what a good idea," said Mckenzie. "What does she need?"

"Everything, I think. They don't have a lot of money, they've been trying to save so she can take time off to be a stay at home mom. I don't know if that's still the plan or if she'll be working here," said David. "Oh new topic; here she comes."

"So, how's the open house coming?" Gina asked Mckenzie.

"Really good. We've got the menu confirmed. And the caterers are happy to make lemonade. They'll make some lavender lemonade too, for people to have something to drink with strawberry tarts. And regular to go with the meal. So thanks for the great idea Shawna."

"Welcome," said Shawna, practically diving into her pasta salad.

"Let the pregnant woman eat," said Gina, laughing.

Shawna swallowed and said, "Oh my god, you should have

seen me last night. I ate half a large Corvid pizza. All by myself. I feel like such a pig these days."

"You need that extra food. Not only for the baby," said David, "but because you've been working extra hard. Lots of overtime like the rest of us. When you should probably be cutting back."

"I need that overtime money," she said. "Gotta build up the emergency fund."

"Have you talked to Cory about working for Taylor's after the baby's born yet?" asked Emily.

"I thought I'd wait till next week. When some of the dust has settled a bit," said Shawna.

"I think you should do it this afternoon. It'll make you feel better. It's not good for you to be so stressed," said David.

"I don't know. He seemed awfully angry this morning."

"Jason and a couple of the others quitting relieved a lot of that," said Mckenzie.

"Okay. I'll try to hunt him down after I eat," said Shawna, shoveling another spoonful of pasta salad in her mouth.

"How's the painting going Gina?" asked Mckenzie.

"I'm not painting today. Still taking photos to catch everything that's going out through Monday morning. Then I'll paint. I'll probably finish the photos after lunch. Then I'm taking myself home to chill out. I'm really tired."

"You need to take care of yourself," said Mckenzie.

David said, "My gram said when she turned sixty that everything shifted for her. She just didn't have the energy that she'd had at forty or even fifty."

"That happened for me," said Gina. "I think it was sixty-two. I'm just done. And there's nothing left until I rest. So, I'll go home and if I have enough oomph, I'll read. If not, then I'll watch a movie. I do need to flatten a few paintings tonight."

"How do you flatten paintings?" asked Emily.

"You stick it between two layers of a clean cotton sheet and iron them. Then weigh them down with books."

"Wow, I would never have thought of that," Emily said.

The talk turned to speculation about how soon the new greenhouses and solar panels might be up. Gina finished her sandwich and went out to the parking lot to put her lunch bag in the car. She decided to leave the chair there. She only had two more plants left to do.

She heard a woman call her name and turned around. It was Sheriff Winters getting out of her SUV. Gina waited.

"How are you today?" the sheriff asked.

"I'm really tired. Besides that, good. I've only got two more types of plants to photograph and then I'm calling it a day."

"I hear there's been some developments this morning."

"Changes yes, I don't know what you heard."

Gina described Cory's talk and about the three men who'd quit.

"Well, that's really generous of him. Two weeks' paid. But I guess that's more and more common these days. It helps get angry and potentially violent people off the property. Having them give two weeks notice and sticking around for that time just leads to temptation for certain personalities."

"I hadn't thought of that," said Gina.

"I thought I'd come poke my nose in and see how things are going," said the Sheriff. "Try to emulate you and ask questions. Talk to people. Be friendly."

"Good for you."

"To quote my son, 'I suck at it.'"

Gina laughed.

"How long did it take you to learn how to be a good enough shot?"

"Years of practice."

"Exactly. You've got to put in the practice. Think of it like that."

"Socializing takes practice?"

"Yes, for some of us. When I was in high school, my best friend was in one of those scholarship pageants, back in the dark ages, not the fancy ones like today. She won Miss Congeniality. Everyone loved her. I'd known her since grade school when she was the shyest person in class. I watched how hard she worked to learn about other kids and then talk to them. It was a real struggle for her at first. But she got better and better. And learned more. She joined clubs and watched the people who were popular. Then she'd analyze what they were doing and copy it. She fell flat several times, but mostly she made friends, good friends."

"Interesting. I've never considered that I might need to practice. Okay, thanks for lesson number one. I owe you a tea and dessert already. Maybe someday next week?"

"Let me make it through this grueling week and I'll see what next week looks like," said Gina.

"Deal," said the Sheriff. "Well, I've gotta sign in at the office and then I'll wander some. See you."

"Good luck," said Gina.

Gina got her photos taken in just an hour and a half. She felt relieved to be done early for the day. She signed out at the office and was home by two.

Albert and Alice shook themselves awake and ran to the kitchen, circling around her legs.

"I know this isn't just because you're happy to see me. But it's not even close to dinnertime, so don't think I'm delusional."

Gina went to her bedroom and changed into a pair of capris and a t-shirt. The day had turned warm and the sun shone into her main room filling it with light. She put her purse away, clipping her keys to the strap. Then tossed her vest into the dirty clothes.

She went into the studio and flattened another painting. Two more to go.

Gina pulled out her black portfolio and opened it. There was nothing in it. She unsnapped the interior strap and laid the already flattened paintings in it, deciding on the order depending on how the colors worked together. Nothing else she could do until they were all ready.

She returned to the main room. The cats followed her around while she tidied up the coffee table and then the kitchen table. They were still hopeful about the whole dinner thing.

Gina poured herself some iced tea and sat in the swivel chair at the end of the coffee table. She turned it to look out at the view and her garden. Then pulled the footstool around and put her feet up and drank the fruity iced tea.

Her garden needed some work. Weeds were coming up through the mulch. And this was almost the time of year to cut back the *Asters* and that tall *Sedum* so they wouldn't get floppy come summer. If she moved the *Geum* over, that might be the perfect spot for that *Heuchera* when she found it at a nursery.

Or maybe she should put it out in the front, in that shady spot that needed something. She should probably wait until after mid-May. Melanie always gave her cool plants for her birthday and whatever her gift was might fill one of those spots.

Still, she should go out and weed. Perhaps this weekend. She'd need to spend some time next week taking photographs. And a lot of time painting.

If Cory, Angie and Mckenzie liked the paintings, she'd have so many paintings to do. She needed to just plug her phone into the computer and directly upload the photos. If she waited for her dodgy Wi-Fi to upload—death from natural causes might arrive sooner.

It felt good to just sit and do nothing. To let her mind wander about the future and what it might hold.

Shelley had said she'd stop by for a couple of weeks after returning from China. She'd need to get another job and knew the guest room was always open for her.

How would her daughters feel about Bryan, if that came to pass? She had no idea. Shelley was the most flexible. Joanna, the least.

Gina's phone rang and she got up to get it.

"Hello."

"How are you?" asked Bryan.

"Good, just sitting around with my feet up."

"Ah, the retired life I long for."

"The life of someone who's been on her feet too much today and who slept badly last night."

"I'm glad to hear things are going well. Just wanted to check in."

"How are things going on your end?"

"Sheriff Winters is still working hard to solve the case, as am I. I think we've come to the same conclusion. There might be an arrest soon, but that's all I can say."

"Good. I'm sure everyone will be relieved by an arrest."

"Yup. Well, I'm off to do policey things."

"Stay safe," she said.

"Always do. You watch out for yourself tomorrow."

"Something happening?" Gina asked.

"Not that I know of."

"Good."

They hung up

Gina had a relaxing evening. She watched a movie, pressed the last two paintings and ate the rest of the leftover pasta with a wonderfully-oaky chardonnay. Then went to bed on time, relaxed and refreshed.

FRIDAY MORNING

GINA WOKE UP TO RAIN POUNDING ON HER ROOF. THE WEATHER had turned. If it stayed rainy all weekend, she wouldn't be out in the garden.

She got up and cooked eggs over easy and toast for breakfast. The cats ate their own breakfast and stared at her. Silently begging for more.

"Nope, nope, nope," she said.

Gina drank her tea, then went to get dressed. Pants, a long-sleeved t-shirt and her waterproof duck shoes. The rain might last or not.

In her studio, she pulled the last painting out from under the drawing board and books. Perfectly flat. She put it between two other paintings in the portfolio. Then snapped the stretchy strap over them to hold all the paintings in place and zipped up the portfolio. She picked it up by the handle and left the studio, closing the door before the cats could get in. They were clearly stalking her.

"I'll be home early today kids. The rain will bring birds out in the garden. Happy watching today. We'll party tonight."

She slid on her raincoat, zipping it up. Grabbed the rain hat, water and purse with her phone in it. Then picked up the portfolio and juggled her way into the garage, taking care to not let the cats in. She checked the interior door, it was locked. Then put everything in the car and opened the large door.

Gina arrived at Taylor Gardens at nine. It was still raining. She put her hat on and took everything with her, locking the car. She went to the office and once inside, shook herself off.

"You're here," said Mckenzie. "None of us could remember when we were meeting."

"I thought it was nine," said Gina.

"Cory said eight, Angie said ten. I didn't know. Great. I'll call Cory. He's out in shipping, talking to people."

"Is there a problem?" asked Gina, taking off her raincoat.

"No more than usual," said Angie, grimacing.

Carla and Emily were there as well, but they remained hard at work on their computers.

One end of the trailer held a round plastic table surrounded by chairs.

Angie pointed to it and said, "Let's meet there, where you can lay out the paintings."

Gina hung up her raincoat and hat from a hook on the wall. She set her water bottle on the table and hung her purse from a chair back. Then tapped the portfolio on the floor to shake some of the water off it.

The door opened and Cory rushed in, as if trying to dodge the rain. He wasn't wearing a coat.

"Gina, good morning. This weather, huh?"

"Yeah. Maybe I don't want to work in my garden tomorrow."

"I heard on the radio a storm's coming in," said Mckenzie

"How big?" asked Angie.

"Big enough," said Mckenzie. "Winds at forty miles an hour maybe."

"That's a lot for a spring storm," said Angie. "Carla, could you pass the word to the field crews?"

"No problem," said Carla. "I need a walk. Stupid internet's out again."

"I'll call this time," said Emily. "Then I'll go tell people in the greenhouses. Hope there's no flying tree branches this time."

Carla went out the door.

Emily got on the phone and began talking to the internet people.

"The big-leaf maples across the street are the worst," said Angie. "But they're not fully leafed out yet. Hopefully they got rid of all their dead branches in that November storm. It was a lot bigger."

Cory said, "Well, that's sorted."

He'd found a hoodie near his desk and was using it to dry his face and hair.

"You're soaked," said Mckenzie.

"I know. Should've worn my raincoat, but I'll dry off."

He sat down in a chair. So did Angie and Mckenzie. Emily went out the door.

Gina unzipped her portfolio, keeping it away from the table, so as not to drip water on it. She didn't want the paintings to run.

She put the stack of paintings on the table and leaned the

portfolio against the wall to drip dry. Then sat down on the plastic chair, scooting it in.

"Oh, I love this one. That *Dicentra*," said Angie. "You've captured it perfectly."

"I love the crown fritillary," said Cory. "They're just the weirdest plants. I think we should plant a whole bunch out by our sign in front. Something to brighten up the dark early spring days."

"If we're picking favorites," said Mckenzie, "I adore this little *Iris*. Such a pretty flower."

"These are all great, Gina. Just what I was looking for," said Cory.

"I agree," said Angie.

"Me three," said Mckenzie.

"Well, thank you. I wish I'd had time to get more painted. But I thought I should keep up with photographing the plants before they were shipped out. I did a couple different styles, so you could choose whether you wanted the labels to be more realistic or to reflect the feeling of the plant when it was mature. And I wasn't sure if you wanted flower details or that entire plant."

"I like both styles," said Angie. "The less precise ones look dreamy, but probably for the plant tags we want precision."

"I agree," said Mckenzie. "But the dreamy ones look wonderful. I think that's the style you should use for some of the marketing material."

"Which ones did you do from the plant and which ones from photos?" asked Cory.

"These are the only two I did from photos." She pointed to them.

"I can't tell the difference," said Angie.

"Me neither," said Cory.

"I'm pleased you like them. Will they work for the tags and labels?"

"Let's see," said Mckenzie. "Can I scan this?" she asked Gina.

"Sure."

"She just wants to play with all the new equipment," teased Angie.

"Yes I do!" said Mckenzie.

She picked up the painting of the *Iris* and went over near her desk. Then opened a lid on one machine and lay the painting face down and fiddled with some controls.

After a minute, the machine stopped. Mckenzie took the painting out and went to her computer. She messed around with it for a few minutes.

Gina drank some water.

"I wanted to talk to you about some of our future plans. Angie said she told you about my idea for a small gift shop in the new office. And you suggested using some of your art for mugs or t-shirts."

"It's just a thought," said Gina. "If you're buying art and paying good money for it, you might want to recoup some of your investment by making merchandise. Angie said you were trying to think of things to sell to tour groups."

"Yeah. We don't want to sell plants, the ones in the greenhouses are pretty much all spoken for. We don't want to have to track individual plant sales. We make more money wholesale with big orders. But people who come to tour here are always asking for stuff. We thought hats or ball caps, t-shirts, maybe aprons, mugs, that sort of stuff. But your idea of putting some of the paintings on sale or using the art on things we sell, that's wonderful. We'd have to find a way to make it fair for you. What do artists usually get for that."

"It's a separate license," said Angie. "If you want to buy the painting for plant tags and labels, that's one license. For merchandise like t-shirts and mugs, that's another license. To buy that painting outright is completely different. Am I right?"

Gina said, "Something like that. I usually just sell the paintings to people. I don't know what they do with it afterwards."

"But they're your creations," said Angie. "You should have some say."

Mckenzie returned with the painting and laid it on the pile. She also had a sheet of paper on which she'd printed a small version of the painting, shrunk down to the size of a pot label and another even smaller, the size of a plant tag photo.

"Oh, these look great," said Cory. "But the color's off."

"That's the new printer," said Mckenzie. "It still needs some adjusting. The company who prints the plant tags and labels will make a better match."

"I love it," said Angie. "It captures all the complexity of the plant."

"I do too," said Cory.

Gina felt relieved.

"So, what would you normally charge for a painting like this," he asked, holding up the fritillary.

"Framed or unframed?" she asked.

"Unframed. I suspect we'd like to take them all and get them framed the same to display them."

"It's small. I think $200.00 is a fair price, considering my time to photograph all the plants needs to be factored in."

"As well as your travel time," said Angie. "And someone

should pay you to put up with us. I think that's a fair price for the painting, but I still feel like we need to pay you extra if we decide to use one for mugs or t-shirts or make prints to sell."

"I agree," said Mckenzie.

"But you're going to be buying hundreds of paintings," said Gina. "Especially if you add in fall and winter plants."

"I agree with Angie," said Cory. "But we won't be making mugs and t-shirts of all those paintings. Just a few. Do you know what those rates might be for special licenses?"

"I have a friend, another artist, I could ask," said Gina.

"Why don't you do that? How about if I start drawing up a contract for selling us the paintings and you can take it to your lawyer and so they can look it over? Then we'll do another one that concerns other usage for the paintings we might want to highlight sometime in the future? Like mugs, t-shirts and whatever. Does that sound good to you?" asked Cory.

"Yes," said Gina.

"And I know I'm going to want to ask you to do other things too. I think we'd probably like some sort of painted garden scene to use on brochures and things. Maybe a painting of our display garden at its peak," said Cory.

"That would be fun," said Angie.

"We could use it on all our marketing," said Mckenzie. "Like a letterhead."

"Would that be all right with you?" asked Cory.

"If I can squeeze it in. If I began painting, from the photographs I've already taken, it might take me till December."

"We don't start shipping until March. So that gives you some extra time, right?" asked Cory, grinning.

"What happened to my retirement?"

"Well, if we don't have your paintings for all the tags, it won't be the end of the world," said Angie.

"She's right," said Cory. "We'd love to have everything perfectly matched, but that's just a goal, not a requirement. Why don't you do what you can, when you can. I'll have the first contract ready for you to look at next week. You can ask your friend about other rates and we can draw up the second one. As soon as the first contract's signed, we'll take the paintings you have done at that time and pay you for them."

"Then you can buy a new phone," said Mckenzie. "So your battery won't be dying all the time."

"I can hardly wait for that," said Gina. "I think it sounds great. But it also sounds like you're paying me too much."

"No, we're not. You've been working just as hard as anyone else the last few days. Don't think I haven't noticed. And you're older than anyone here. Those are long days you've been putting in. Your paintings are worth every penny. I think you're giving them to us too cheaply. Although I'm also glad they're affordable, since there's going to be so many," said Cory.

"Exactly," said Mckenzie.

Angie nodded.

The trailer door flung open and someone came in behind Gina.

"Close the door please," said Angie, turning around.

"None of you can ever tell me what to do again."

Gina turned around.

It was Jason and he had a handgun.

She slid her hand into her purse. Pulled her phone out, keeping it out of sight. Gina dialed 911.

"You all should have been drowned at birth!" yelled Jason.

"Jason, we can talk about this," said Cory.

"I'm done talking!" Jason yelled.

911 answered. They asked a question that she couldn't hear. Gina had the volume turned way down, so Jason couldn't hear it.

"I'm tired of being a second-class citizen in this place!" Jason yelled.

The 911 operator said, "If it's not safe to answer, please stay on the line. We're tracing your call."

Gina hoped the nearest cell tower was close. She didn't dare talk on the phone.

Her heart was pounding and she forced herself to breathe. Mckenzie's face was white. Cory was listening intently to Jason. Angie sat clutching her fists. It looked like she wanted to kill him.

Gina could smell the alcohol on his breath from where she sat. He staggered a bit, obviously drunk.

"You were all promoted when I shoulda been. Wet under the ears. I had the experience! I gave a decade of my life to this company before you were even born. And your little brother, what a waste of space!"

Jason's voice got louder louder as he yelled to be heard over the wind. The door was still open

"Your Dad shoulda given me credit for all the work I did. What did he give me? A piddly raise. I shoulda been moved up to management!"

He began shooting. Cory hit the floor behind a desk. Gina followed Mckenzie who dropped to the floor. Gina awkwardly crawled around to the far side of the table by the door, still holding her phone. Her knees screamed with every movement.

Jason was still yelling. Gina could see his feet and legs

beneath the table. His attention was turned to Cory.

She whispered into her phone.

"Help. Taylor Gardens. Police and ambulance. We have a shooter."

"Police are on their way," said the operator. "Stay on the line if you can."

Jason kept yelling about being a manager. And shooting.

Cory was yelling. Sounds, not words.

Gina felt her body shaking with fear. She couldn't control it.

Should she try to make it to the door and out?

Gina heard heavy footsteps and voices.

"Police! Drop the weapon!"

She didn't recognize the voice.

Then there was a heavy thud.

Jason was still yelling.

Gina realized her eyes were closed. She opened them, remembering to breathe again.

Jason was writhing on the floor, covered with one of two, black clad bodies. Had they gotten the gun away from him? Was Cory all right?

Then Sheriff Jannson said, "Get him out of here."

Sirens sounded outside. An ambulance?

She hadn't heard the police sirens. They must not have used them.

Gina saw Angie stand up.

"Is he gone?"

"Yes, it's safe now," said Sheriff Jannson.

"Cory," said Angie, in an anguished voice.

"I'm okay. But I think he got me in the arm. I'm bleeding."

Angie rushed over and so did the sheriff.

More feet came in through the doorway. Gina recognized the EMTs' uniforms.

"Over here," said Sheriff Winters.

"Back here," said Angie. "My brother's been shot."

Sheriff Jannson came over near the table.

"Everybody else okay? Gina, are you okay?" he asked, spotting her.

"I'm fine. Just scared out of my wits."

"Understandable," he said.

He held out his hands to help her up. Gina stood and he helped her onto a chair. It was pouring down rain outside still. His clothes and hair were drenched.

Mckenzie had gotten up and was watching the EMTs work on Cory. They were putting him on a stretcher.

More EMTs came to the door.

Sheriff Jannson talked to them and one of them came over to Gina, the other to Mckenzie.

The EMT put a blanket around Gina's shoulders. She was still shaking, but not from cold.

"Is this your water," the woman asked, lifting Gina's water bottle.

Gina nodded, reaching for it with a shaky arm. She sipped some water. She wasn't thirsty, but holding her water bottle and drinking felt comforting.

The EMT began to ask her medical history questions. Gina answered the questions while watching as they carried Cory out. He was awake, but his face looked strained.

Angie was putting her coat on and grabbing her cane, purse and phone all at once.

"I'm going in the ambulance. I'll need someone to pick me up later. Or something."

Mckenzie said, "Someone will give you a ride back here. Don't worry. I'm sure Emily will get everything under control. Call and let us know how Cory is."

"I will."

After they left, Sheriff Jannson asked, "Is there somewhere we can go to talk, so Sheriff Winters can collect evidence here?"

Mckenzie said, "We can go into the next trailer. It's the break room."

"Let's do that," he said. "Gina are you up for going for a walk?"

"Yes. Should I put my paintings away?"

"Why don't you wait till you return? Just get your coat and purse and phone. I'm sure Sheriff Winters and the deputies will be careful of your paintings."

"Yes, we will," said Sheriff Winters. "Go on. You'll feel better if you get out of here."

"The paintings can't get wet," said Gina.

"Understood," said Sheriff Winters.

Gina stood up, taking the blanket off and handing it to the EMT. Then put on her raincoat and hat, got her purse and water bottle and picked up her phone off the floor. She turned it off.

Sheriff Jannson took her by the arm as they walked to the next trailer, following Mckenzie. Emily and Carla were already there, making coffee.

"What can I get you, Gina?" asked Emily.

"Black tea, with cream or milk or something," she said.

"Done. We've got cream. Angie uses it."

Gina sat at the table. It was warmer in this trailer. They'd turned the heat on and the door hadn't been left open.

Sheriff Jannson began asking Mckenzie questions first. Emily brought Gina the hot tea and sat down near her, putting her arm around Gina's shoulders.

"I'm so glad they caught him," said Emily. "I hope this is the end of this."

"Me too," said Gina.

After he finished with Mckenzie, Sheriff Jannson asked Gina a few questions.

"How are you feeling?"

"Better. I don't think I've been so afraid in my whole life."

"That's because you're smart. Do you have anyone to take you home?"

"I can't leave my car here."

"Sure you can. Leave the car keys with me and I'll have one of the deputies bring it by later. You need to go home. You're in shock."

"Melanie's working today. I could call her though." Gina separated the car fob from her house keys. She handed it to him.

"I'll give you a ride," he said. "I need to get back to the station anyway and begin interviewing the prisoner. There's more than enough of us here."

Gina nodded.

"I'll go collect your paintings. Give me about five minutes and then come out."

"Okay. I feel so wimpy."

"You're not wimpy. None of you are. You've just been through a horrible situation. One none of you signed up for. Be kind to yourself. You should go home too, Mckenzie."

"I'll call Steph. She has the day off.

He got up and left the trailer.

"Angie's going to need a ride back here from the hospital. She'll need her car," said Mckenzie to Emily.

"I'll find someone and have them call her," said Emily.

"And please call me and let me know how Cory is."

"I will."

"Me too, if you've got time," said Gina.

"I'll be fine. Boss for a day! Whee! Everything will be fine. We've only got about three hours left here anyway. There's no late shipping today. So we'll shut things down at three. Did Cory leave his keys?"

"Here, take mine," said Mckenzie. "You can give them back on Monday."

Gina finished her tea and stood up to go wash the cup.

"I'll do that," said Carla.

"Oh, thank you."

She hadn't taken off the raincoat but put on her rain hat. Then picked up her purse and water bottle.

"I'll see all of you, probably Monday."

"Are you sure?" asked Mckenzie. "You might want to take more time off."

"I'll have all weekend off. And I need to take more photos on Monday. Before the plants leave. Keep me posted on Cory please."

"We will. You go home and take care of yourself," said Emily.

"Thanks, I will."

Gina went outside, into the still pouring rain. The region's rivers would be flooding if this kept up. Wind threatened to blow her hat off, so she tightened the toggle on the strap.

Sheriff Jannson was standing just inside the open door of

the office trailer, talking to Sheriff Winters. He spotted her and came outside.

He took her arm and walked her to his SUV. He helped her in and put her portfolio in the back. Then got in.

"How are you feeling?"

"I'll be fine."

"Hungry?"

She had to think about it. Her stomach felt upset, but it was past lunchtime.

"I should eat something."

"How about some clam chowder from the Marina?"

"That sounds perfect, but I don't want to go to a restaurant."

"I'll call an order in and we can take it to your house to eat."

"Oh, that would be great. I couldn't face Misty."

"I can. I never tell her anything, so she's quit asking me questions."

He called in an order and drove through downtown to the Marina. After parking, he got out and went inside to get the food, leaving her to sit in the warm vehicle, the motor running.

At her house, he parked in her driveway and they went in through the front door. The cats barely looked up. Gina hung up her dripping wet hat and coat. Then propped up her portfolio in the mudroom area to drip dry. Luckily, she'd planned well and bought the waterproof version rather than a leather one. Her paintings would stay dry inside it.

Bryan was already unpacking the food on her kitchen table. He got silverware from the drawer and set it on the table.

Then he put his arms around her and held her for a good

long while. Gina felt like she'd melted into a pile of goo. It was shocking to realize how much she needed to be held.

She wiped the tears from her face, feeling the pressure in her chest.

"You okay?" he asked.

"Yes. It's been a long, long time since I was held like that. I really needed it today."

"Good. Pleased to be of service. I plan on being around a lot more in the future. And giving you a hug anytime you need one."

"I think that would be quite wonderful."

She sat down at the table and stared at the food.

"Eat," he said. "Unless you want me to feed you."

Gina shook herself and picked up a spoon. The soup tasted wonderful. Creamy and warm. It hadn't sounded good, but actually, was just what she needed. She ate half of the container but couldn't finish it.

"I got fish sandwiches too."

"I don't think I can eat that much. I can't even finish the soup."

"Well, I'll put yours in the fridge. Stick it into the microwave for a minute and a half and it'll still be terrific," he said.

Gina nodded.

He got up and put the leftover soup in her fridge. Then washed the silverware. He put the teakettle on and pulled a mug out of her cupboard.

"Thank you," she said.

"You're welcome. I wish I could stay, but there's still a lot to do."

"Of course," she said. "You should go."

"First, I'll make you a cup of tea. How about some chamomile?"

"I think I'll have mint instead."

"Done."

He made her a cup of tea and set it in front of her.

"Call Melanie."

"I will."

"Now, please."

He handed her the phone, which she'd plugged in to charge.

Gina called Melanie who offered to come over and bring dinner.

"What do you want?" asked Melanie.

"Mexican," Gina said.

"I'll be there around five."

"Thank you," said Gina, clicking the phone off.

She said, "Okay, I called her."

"Now I want you to drink your tea and do something relaxing. Deputy Hammond said she'd bring your car back later this afternoon."

"Oh, that's wonderful."

"And I'll check in when I can," he said. "Until then, relax."

Gina's phone rang.

"Hello."

"Gina, this is Emily. Cory's out of surgery. He was hit in the upper arm. They got the bullet out and have him bandaged up. He's doing fine but won't be using that arm soon. They won't know the extent of the damage for a bit, but the bullet seems to have missed anything major. Angie's coming back in an hour or two."

"Oh good, thank you for calling."

"You're welcome. Well, I'd better get back to work."

"See you next week."

"Yes. Bye," said Emily.

Gina clicked the phone off.

"It looks like Cory's going to be all right."

"Good. Well I'll be going now."

"Do you think Jason was responsible for all these things?"

"I think he's partly responsible."

"So, there's someone else?"

"I believe so. I'm going to go find out. Lock the door after I leave, please."

"I'm not at risk, am I?"

"I don't think you are. I still think the Taylors are the targets. But I think you should lock your front door all the time and I was afraid you'd forget today."

"You're right, I had. I guess I'm still more rattled than I thought."

"Do you need someone to be here when I leave?"

"No, I'm not that upset. Go. Do your work and catch whoever it is. If you have time, could you let me know when you've arrested everyone."

He nodded and left, his face grim. Gina locked the door. She wandered around the house for a couple of minutes. Taking off her shoes and putting on cozy slippers. It was a bit chilly, so she got out her favorite fuzzy gray cardigan.

Then she took her portfolio into the studio. Someone had neatly put the paintings inside, fastening the strap. Gina pulled them out, to make certain none were missing. She set them in a pile and left the portfolio leaning against a file cabinet so it would dry completely.

She went back out into the main room and flipped on the

tv. Bringing her mug over to the couch, she sat down, putting her feet up on the coffee table. Albert came over and sat on her lap. Alice curled up beside her. Before long, the duo was purring happily.

Gina watched a special edition of the Seattle news. There was lots of flooding and it was still raining, although a little less than this morning. The winds were still up and the news said they expected it to die down after ten tonight.

She hoped there wouldn't be any storm losses. A lot of people had lost power, as was usual with storms in this area. It's why Ewan had demanded they get a house with a wood stove.

Gina surfed through the channels, restlessly looking for something entertaining.

And waiting for news.

SATURDAY MORNING

G INA SLEPT LATE THE NEXT MORNING. U NTIL NINE. S HE'D LEFT food out for the cats last night, so they wouldn't wake her up early.

She felt groggy.

Melanie had come over last night with a feast of food from La Cantina. Then they talked and watched fluffy movies.

Bryan called around eight to check on her. He either didn't have any news or couldn't tell her anything. Gina suspected things hadn't been resolved.

She had no real plans for today. Earlier in the week, she'd thought to spend the day painting. But after yesterday, she just didn't want to.

Even after spending last night doing nothing, it's what she wanted to do today.

Gina heated up tea water and her eye caught the box of pastries from Corr's that Melanie had brought last night. She opened it and put a cream cheese Danish on a plate. Sprinkled a few drops of water on it and stuck it in the microwave. Melanie knew her better than she knew herself.

Gina sat with her mug of Earl Grey tea and the Danish, looking out the window. She had soft Celtic fiddle music playing. Outside it was bright and sunny, the storm had blown through and left everything fresh and clean.

She was still in her pajamas when there was a knock at the front door. Gina smoothed her hair down and went to look through the peephole. It was Melanie.

"Come in," Gina said, holding the door open.

"I brought lunch. I know you haven't been shopping in a while."

"It seems like I barely finished breakfast," said Gina.

"They'll keep. And I brought more movies." Melanie held up a tote bag that looked stuffed.

"Oh, are we doing more movies today?"

"You got plans?"

"Not a one. I don't want to do anything today."

"But movies are okay?"

"Movies are perfect. How did you know?"

"I'm just that good," said Melanie, laughing.

She unpacked the food bags on the table. Gina didn't recognize the packaging.

"Where did you go?"

"There's a new place, Taste of the Raj. Just opened this week. Thought we should try it out before it's gone."

"You never know, it might stay."

Restaurants came and went so quickly. Opened by people with dreams and culinary skills, but not enough business sense to make a go of things in a tough economy.

"I got all the appetizers. Samosas and pakoras and all sorts of things I can't remember. I just got one order of every appetizer and oh, here's their menu."

"Wonderful," said Gina.

She hadn't been hungry until Melanie began opening the boxes. The smells were intoxicating and exotic.

"Shall I make some tea to go with things?" asked Gina.

"Got it," said Melanie, holding up a container. "Just fill each mug half full of this, and half of milk and nuke."

Gina followed the instructions and soon they were sitting at the table eating. The flavors were as astounding as the scents. She had no idea what half of them were, even after reading the menu.

"This food is wonderful. We have to go there."

"I agree," said Melanie. "I hope they survive."

They were halfway through an adaptation of Pride and Prejudice when there was another knock at the door. Deputy Hammond stood there.

"I'm sorry, I couldn't get your car brought over yesterday. I hope it didn't inconvenience you," she said.

Gina put her hand over her mouth.

"I totally forgot. No inconvenience at all. I just wanted to stay home."

"Good," said the Deputy.

"Any news yet?" asked Gina.

"Sheriff Jannson said he'd give you a call later today. We've been crazy busy, between all this and problems caused by the storm."

"Problems?"

"There's some flooding near Tapwater Creek. Road closed, so we've got someone directing traffic and a couple other people making sure folks there evacuate."

"Oh dear. I hope everyone's all right."

A police SUV pulled up.

"Well, I better get going, there's my ride," said the Deputy.

"Thanks again," said Gina.

She closed the door and locked it.

"That was Deputy Hammond, bringing my car back. I can't believe that I didn't even realize she didn't bring it yesterday."

"You were a bit stressed."

"I'm going to put it in the garage."

"Okay. I'll go use the facilities while you do that."

Gina went out to the garage and put her car inside. She was feeling a little protective of the new car.

She went back inside and they watched more of the movie while eating some coconut cake Melanie had brought last night. The cats joined in the party, each having a lap.

Just as the movie ended, there was another knock on the door.

Gina looked through the peephole. Sheriff Jannson.

She opened the door.

"Come in."

"Is Melanie here? That's her pickup, right?"

"Yes. She's applying the fluffy movies and food treatment."

He laughed.

"I can talk about what's been going on if you have time."

"Yes please. Are you off duty? We were about to move onto the wine portion of our entertainment."

"I'd love a small glass of wine. But I haven't slept in too long to have more."

"You didn't sleep last night?"

He shook his head.

"Well come in and sit down. I'll open the wine. There's still some Indian food on the table."

"From the new place? I've wanted to try it but haven't been able to get there when they were open. Hi Melanie."

"Hi. You've brought us news?"

He sat at the table and began eating the finger food. Melanie sat down as well.

"This is incredible," he said.

Gina pulled the Semillon from the fridge and opened it. Then got out three glasses. She poured one for Melanie and herself and handed Bryan the bottle.

"I'll let you pour your own, so you get the right amount."

He poured a small amount and sipped it, his eyes closed. She sat and sipped her wine, watching him take a deep breath.

"Okay. Well, a lot has been going on behind the scenes that I haven't been able to talk about. So I'll start at the beginning. Jason wasn't the only one involved here. He was just the obvious person. John Martin has been behind all of this."

"John, John from shipping?"

"Yes. He was also passed over for advancement and was bitter about it. He felt he'd given everything to the company after revolutionizing their shipping department. He saw others were angry about things too, so he put together a plan. Carlos Martinez was a wild card. After he killed Dustin, John and Jason decided to act."

So Carlos wasn't part of this?" asked Gina.

"No. He was just furious at Dustin for getting his daughter pregnant. And then dumping her."

"Wow."

"So Jason sawed the line of hanging baskets, weakening it. He had Trang messing with the water lines that same morning, knowing that would throw suspicion on him. Trang quit after realizing that Jason tried to frame him. He didn't want to work with him anymore. He couldn't be sure if Jason was trying to kill Angie or just injure her, but it made him mad."

"What was Jason trying to do?" asked Melanie.

"Kill her. Even though he'd spent years working with her, he still hated her for being promoted over him. After that attempt failed, Jason got scared and laid low for awhile. John was furious. And taking it out on everyone he worked with."

"Now that I heard about," said Gina.

"The propane tanks were enclosed in a locked fence, a cage really. The fire investigators couldn't find that anyone tampered with the tanks. The explosion came from within the building.

"Last night, Jason admitted to cutting a hole in the gas lines inside the shipping area. Hoping it would take Cory out, along with his office.

"But Cory was working off-site that morning. The only injuries were in shipping. Which put more pressure on John. He either had to come clean or pretend he wanted the business to keep going. Or leave. He wasn't willing to give up access to the Taylors. That would make revenge more difficult.

"So he was stuck trying to work twice as hard in the new shipping spot, trying to get caught up. Which made him almost rabid.

"He and Jason had a big argument in the parking lot the other day. Which you saw part of."

"I wondered who John was fighting with," said Gina.

"It was Jason. They were trying to figure out how to kill both Cory and Angie at once. They'd used up their big idea, the gas explosion. John overheard about your meeting with Cory and Angie and told Jason. Jason showed up yesterday, determined to kill both of them, but not really caring if anyone else was in the way. At the same time, John was on his way to break into Bob's house last night and poison all his hard liquor."

"Bob was always fond of a drink," said Melanie.

"So you've arrested both of them?" asked Gina.

"Yes. We've released Trang, since he wasn't part of this. And Carlos, of course, remains in custody. He won't be released."

"So, it's all done," said Gina.

"Our part is as done as it can be for now."

"How many days since you've slept?" asked Melanie.

"Might be a couple," grinned Bryan.

"Then you need to get to bed."

"I needed to come here. Talk it out and wind down a bit. Home and bed are next on my agenda. Plus, I needed this exquisite food. Sorry to eat your dinner."

"It was our lunch," said Gina. "And we were done. Melanie bought an enormous amount of food."

"Yesterday was payday and it's our busy shipping season too, so I've had plenty of overtime. Where better to spend it than on you? The grandkids don't need more toys, much as I love them," said Melanie.

There was another knock at the door.

"Well, you are the popular person today," said Melanie.

Gina looked through the peephole. It was Sheriff Winters. She opened the door.

"Come on in."

"It looks like you've already got a party going," the Sheriff said. She came in followed by Elijah who carried two large Corvid pizza boxes.

"Hello Bryan." And then to Melanie, "I'm Ivy and this is my son, Elijah."

"Nice to meet you, I'm Melanie."

Bryan was taking the empty food boxes off the table and putting them into the garbage.

"Congratulations on solving your first case here," said Gina.

"Thank you. I couldn't have done it without Bryan. And you."

"Me, I couldn't have been any help," said Gina.

"You were. If you hadn't given me hints about how to talk to people, I wouldn't have walked around the greenhouses trying to do it. So, I was practicing and that's when people began to talk to me about what they knew. Without that, I'd still be sitting at my desk trying to figure things out in my head. I don't know how I survived in Chicago."

"You probably did what most cops do," said Bryan. "Rely on other cops with better people skills."

"You're right. That's probably what I did. I was lucky there."

Melanie smiled and nodded towards the couch. Gina looked. Elijah was already sitting on the couch with both cats on his lap, purring.

"You happy, Elijah?" she asked.

"Yes. Mom says Auntie's moving out here soon and we're going to get a house together. So I'll get to live with cats. I can't wait."

"Well, I don't know about you, but I'm starving," said Ivy. "It was my turn to pay. I've got one Garlic Lovers with Canadian Bacon and one Meaty Magic. So dish up."

Bryan had set a stack of plates on the counter by the open pizza boxes.

"Would you like some wine, Ivy?"

"Maybe just a glass. I'm off till tomorrow morning."

Melanie, Elijah, Ivy and Gina dished up and sat down. Bryan remained standing.

"I think I'm going to take myself home and fall into bed," he said. "The lack of sleep will hit in about half an hour."

"Can you make it home all right?" asked Gina.

"I'll be fine. But not if I stay longer."

She walked him to the front door.

"Thank you for taking the time to stop and fill me in."

"It was my pleasure. It's nice to see the relief on your face."

"Nice to feel the relief."

"I'll touch base tomorrow."

"Only if you're conscious."

He nodded and left. She locked the door behind him and returned to the table.

"I'm still planning on taking you out for dessert and tea," said Ivy. "Don't think I forgot about it just because this whole thing blew up last night and today."

"I did forget," said Gina.

"You had good cause," said Ivy.

Ivy turned to Melanie and said, "Somewhere along the line, when people skills were handed out, I was off doing something else. So, Gina's teaching me how to talk to people."

"She's a good teacher," said Melanie. "Once she even tried to teach me how to paint plants. But apparently you have to practice. So that was the end of that."

Ivy laughed.

"How's school?" Gina asked Elijah.

"It's good. I have some friends now. People are friendlier out here than Chicago. And they have stuff in common with me. The same movies, same music."

"It's good to have friends," said Gina.

She felt rich with friends.

Gina only had one piece of pizza, but it was rich and spicy from the sausage. Just perfect.

They sat around and talked for a couple of hours, then Ivy and Elijah went home. Gina convinced them to take half the leftovers.

Melanie left soon afterwards. She'd had her own busy week, just not as stressful.

Gina headed to bed early, feeling completely exhausted from doing nothing.

SUNDAY MORNING

GINA WAS HAVING TEA AND STARING OUT AT THE GARDEN. IT WAS
mid-morning. Should she work out in the garden today?

She had a ton of laundry to do. And some cleaning. None
of which appealed to her. At least she'd changed out of her
pajamas this morning.

Her phone rang. Gina didn't recognize the number and it
wasn't a local area code, but she answered anyway, expecting a
telemarketer.

"Hello."

"Gina? This is Sandra Wells."

"Hello Sandra. How are you?"

"Better than yesterday. It's been pretty stressful. I'm sure
you heard about Cory."

"Yes, how's he doing?"

"Well, he's still in the hospital. They're letting him out
today. He's his usual joking self. Claims he's beginning a new
diet. That it turns out being overweight is a benefit. The bullet
hit on a fatty area on his arm, because there was quite a lot of

it, and didn't do much other damage. Eventually, he'll have full use of his arm and hand. Once it stops hurting so much."

Gina laughed.

"Well, I guess he's looking on the bright side."

"Yes. So my family's safe. They've arrested the troublemakers and have a good case against them. They should be going to jail for a long time, I hope."

"Good."

"I was calling to see if you have any time to meet for coffee or lunch or something next week. I'm longing to talk about something other than my family and plants. If the timing isn't right, no worries. I've given Cory and Angie a loan to get rebuilding started, so I'll be up regularly to check on my investment."

"I'd love to," said Gina. "I can probably swing lunch on Thursday. What sounds interesting seafood or Indian?"

"Indian, definitely. I've been to the Marina three times already since I got here."

"I have the perfect place. I'll need to look up the address and I'll text you. Noon?"

"Perfect," said Sandra. "See you then."

Gina put it on the calendar on her phone. And on the one hanging in the kitchen.

There was a knock on her door. She looked through the peephole. Bryan, looking much better than he had yesterday.

She opened the door and he came in. Gina closed and locked the door.

"Hello, you're looking rested."

"I slept ten hours. Haven't done that in a while. Had to get up after that. Too sore."

He was wearing jeans and a blue t-shirt. It still felt strange to see him out of uniform. Most of the time she'd known him, he wore it.

"I have some news," he said.

"More news?"

"I'm retiring in two weeks."

"So soon?" she asked.

"It seems like an eternity to me."

"I'll bet. So Ivy's taking your job for sure? It sounded like it last night."

"Yes. As of today, I'm stepping back and just tying up any loose ends. I won't be out on the roads. Just doing paperwork. And then I'm done, except for a couple of trials I'll need to testify at. But most of my time will be my own. And yours, of course."

So this was it. The point she'd been waiting for.

"Well, it'll be interesting to see how it works out between us."

He cocked his head, "You don't think it will?"

"I think it will. I just don't know how."

"I'm willing to take things as slow or as fast as you want. You're driving this car. I'm just coming along for the ride."

"That's not what I want," she said.

"What do you want?"

"A partner. A co-pilot. Someone who's willing to take an equal share of the load."

"I'm that guy," said Bryan, grinning. "I'll do whatever it takes to make this work. You have my full attention."

Gina smiled. This was going to be an interesting change in her life. One she welcomed with open arms.

DICENTRA SPECTABILIS '*GOLD HEART*' (BLEEDING HEART) - Introduced in 1997 by Hadspen Garden in Somerset, England. It was found as a brightly-colored seedling of *Dicentra spectabilis*. Bleeding hearts contain toxic alkaloids that can cause nausea, seizures and breathing issues.

Fritillaria imperialis (Crown Fritillary) - ranges from Kurdistan through Turkey, Iraq, Iran, Afghanistan, Pakistan and the foothills of the Himalayas. Naturalized in some areas - Washington state! The smell is possibly a mouse and mole repellent. (Must try this and see if it makes my moles move elsewhere!)

Fritillaria meleagris (Snake's Head Fritillary, checkered lily, guinea hen flower,) - native to river flood plains in Europe. Genus name is from the Latin - dice box, in reference to the checkered pattern on the petals of this species. Guinea hen flower is because of the spots, like a guinea hen.

Anemone nemorosa (Windflower) from the Greek anemos - wind, daughter of the wind. Woodland plant, long lived.

Sometimes used to date old woodlands in Great Britain by how large the colony is. Native to Northern Europe. In the buttercup family.

Heuchera 'Topaz Jazz' (Coral Bells) - Heuchera are native to North America and Mexico. Topaz Jazz was introduced by Dan Heims of Terra Nova in Oregon. The genus is named after Johann Heinrich Heucher, an Austrian professor of medicine and botany. He was a friend of Linnaeus, who began this whole labeling of plants in Latin and named many of them after his friends. Heuchera were used by some Native Americans to stop bleeding, thus the common name Alum root. (Apparently, *Heuchera* leaves can live up to two years in a vase. Will have to try this out in my next flower arrangement!) Related to our native *Tiarella* (foamflower).

Iris reticulata 'Katharine Hodgkin' (netted iris) - The genus iris is named after the Greek Goddess of the rainbow. This species is native to Turkey, Iraq, Iran and Russia. Introduced in 1958 by E.B. Anderson and named after the wife of passionate gardener, Eliot Hodgkin. A cross between *Iris winogradowii* and *Iris histrioides*. (What was it about Katharine Hodgkin that inspired this naming? She was the mother of Howard Hodgkin and she and her son left England, evacuating to Long Island during WW2. No mention of Eliot going with them.)

Epimedium 'Pink Champagne' (elf orchid, fairy wings, horny goat weed) - mostly native to China, also other parts of Asia and the Mediterranean region. *Epimedium* is used in Chinese medicine to treat erectile disfunction, bone problems and other health issues. The parentage of this variety is *E. leptorrhizum X E. pubescens*. Hybridized by Darrel Probst of Massachusetts. Deer resistant and long lived.

Osteospermum (African Daisy) - native to Africa. Named

from the Greek osteon (bone) and Latin spermum (seed). Likely parentage is *O. ecklonis, E. jucundum* and several other species. So many varieties!

Begonia rex (Painted-leaf *Begonia*, Rex *Begonia*) Native to the forests of northern India. The genus *Begonia* is named after Michael Begon (1638-1710), a Governor of French Canada. (Did Linnaeus know him too?)

Gazania rigens (Treasure flower, African Daisy) - Native to South Africa and Mozambique. Genus name possibly comes from Theodore de Gaza, a 15th. century Greek scholar who translated botanical works into Latin. Also possibly from the Latin - gaza - meaning treasure. Rigens means stiff or rigid. Part of the aster family.

Calibrachoa (Million Bells)- Native to South America, specifically Brazil, Peru and Chile. There they grow on cliff edges and rocky scree. Once a part of the genus *Petunia*, both of which are in the nightshade family. Came on the U.S. market in the late '80s, their popularity exploded in the '90s.

Thank you for reading. I hope you enjoyed visiting with Gina and her friends. If you would be kind enough to leave a review on Amazon or Goodreads, I'd really appreciate it. Even simple one-line reviews help other readers find books they might like. Thanks you so much!

Linda Jordan

Linda Jordan writes fascinating characters, visionary worlds, and imaginative fiction. She creates both long and short fiction, serious and silly. She believes in the power of healing and transformation, and many of her stories follow those themes.

In a previous lifetime, Linda coordinated the Clarion West Writers' Workshop as well as the Reading Series. She spent four years as Chair of the Board of Directors during Clarion West's formative period. She's also worked as a travel agent, a baker, and a pond plant/fish sales person, you know, the sort of things one does as a writer.

Currently, she's the Programming Director for the Writers Cooperative of the Pacific Northwest.

Linda now lives in the rainy wilds of Washington state with her husband, daughter, four cats, a cluster of Koi and an infinite number of slugs and snails.

Her other work includes:

~Horticultural Homicide: A Gina Wetherby Mystery

~Poison Passion: A Gina Wetherby Mystery

~Continental Divide

~Bibi's Bargain Boutique

All her work can be found at your favorite online bookseller.

Get a FREE ebook!

Sign up for Linda's Serendipitous Newsletter at her website: www.LindaJordan.net

She can be found on Facebook at:

www.facebook.com/LindaJordanWriter

Metamorphosis Press website is at:

www.MetamorphosisPress.com

Goodreads: https://www.goodreads.com/author/show/2021274.Linda_Jordan

Writers love reviews, even short, simple ones. Honest reviews help other readers find the book. Please go to where you bought this book, or Goodreads, and leave a review. It would be much appreciated.